Contents

Contents

1

DISCOVERY

IT IS ON nights like this that I remember: cold, bitter nights, with the stars hard and sharp and brilliant, spelling out their patterns across the skies. Then I walk the Cliffs of Moher watching the night sky above the towering cliffs, listening to the wild western seas pound against the rocks ... and I remember.

It was a night like this that the Small Folk came to the Land of Erin in the metal ships of the Tuatha De Danann. It seems like only yesterday, and yet it is so long ago that even the stars have moved a little in the heavens. As humans measure time, that was many thousands of years ago ... but the Small Folk are long-lived, and I have lived longer than most.

For I am Seamus Ban, King of the Leprechauns ...

The Leprechauns came to the tiny island that would one day grow into the Land of Erin when the world was young. We travelled across the vast western sea from the land of the De Danann folk. We had been forced to flee the island when ground started shifting and moving. Then, in a single night, mountains which spat fire and boiling mud had burst up from the sea bed, the seas had risen and the waters had turned to boiling. Many of the De Danann folk believed that they had angered their terrible goddess, the Lady Danu, but no one knew how or why, and so they locked themselves away to pray and offer sacrifices to her, leaving the day-to-day running of the island to us, their servants, the Small Folk, the Leprechauns.

The Small Folk, who knew the ways of the wind and waves, the patterns of the earth and rivers, knew that the islands of the De Danann were threatened with destruction. My people, the Small Folk, had been expecting it. We had seen the tiny wisps of smoke appear from the volcanoes which surrounded the four cities. These fire-mountains had not erupted for many hundreds of years. The De Danann thought they were dead and extinct, but the Small Folk knew that they had been merely sleeping. We had watched all the animals leave the cities in the days before the earth had shifted. We had noted how the fishermen had come back with smaller and smaller catches, and how the birds which usually nested on the cliff faces hadn't returned to their roosts that year.

And so, while the People of the Goddess huddled in their cellars and temples, praying to their Goddess, the Leprechauns had loaded up the huge metal ships with goods and tools, with sacks of grain, dried meat and hard bread, with healing herbs and the seed of rare trees and bushes, and a few of the ancient books and charts of the De Danann.

But when the Small Folk went for our masters and mistresses, we found that few of the Tuatha De Danann would heed our advice, preferring to place their trust in the Goddess Danu. They told us that she would not allow the island to be destroyed.

A few did believe us however – barely enough to fill four ships – and these sailed away just in time. For, even as they reached the horizon, the Isle of the De Danann was completely destroyed as an explosion tore it in half like a piece of cloth, and turned the day into night with a towering cloud of black smoke. The sea then rushed in, covered the shattered remnants of the isle, and the smouldering volcanoes suddenly erupted, covering everything in a thick blanket of seething lava. In less than the time it takes to tell, the De Danann Isle was completely destroyed, and many thousands of years of magic and learning were lost.

We sailed with the De Danann for seven days and seven nights, and during the days the skies were darkened by smoke and the air was filthy with choking volcanic dust, the sun lost behind the racing clouds. At night the stars were invisible and when the moon did appear, it was red and angry purple. The Tuatha De Danann, who were tall and thin, and very beautiful, were terrified: the dirty air burned their lungs, their large eyes were red with grit and their pale skins were raw and blotchy. So they were forced to remain in their cabins below decks, leaving the control of the craft to us, their servants.

My father Niall was King of the Leprechauns then. He was the oldest of the Small Folk, some said the oldest creature in the world, and certainly, he had walked the world in the Time of the Dragons before the first humans had appeared. He was taller than most of the Small Folk, his back was straight, his hair and beard were snow white, and only his face, which was a mass of wrinkles, betrayed his great age.

On the morning of the fifth day out from the Isle of the De Danann, Niall called his sons together. The king had two sons, but they were step-brothers and didn't look in the least like each other. My step-brother was Gilla, whose mother had been from the Fir Dearg, the Red Folk tribe: he was small and red-faced with a large bulbous nose and a mass of red hair and freckles. His clothing was of differing shades of red and bronze and his temper was as quick and as fierce as his clothing.

And then there was me, Seamus Ban. My mother had been Niall's second wife, and she had been from the Leprechaun tribe, which made me a full-blooded Leprechaun. At that time, I was tall and thin – though still no taller than a De Danann child – and although my hair is now white, at that time, it was coal black.

Gilla and I found our father standing in the prow of the boat, his left arm wrapped around the neck of the huge dragon-shaped figurehead, his right hand shading his eyes as he peered through the shifting clouds of fog and dust that had surrounded the ships since the De Danann isle had sunk beneath the waves. I stood on my father's right-hand side, while Gilla took up the position on his left.

Without looking at either of us, Niall spoke very softly: 'We must find land soon, our supplies cannot last much longer.'

He suddenly turned around and leaned with his back against the figurehead, his arms folded across his barrel-chest. He looked at each of us in turn and when

10

he spoke again, his voice was low and serious. 'You know that there will come a day when I will leave this world and go on the last great journey that every living creature makes. I am no longer young, and that day draws ever nearer. I must choose a successor – I must decide which one of you will be King of the Small Folk, King of the Leprechauns.'

'I am the first born,' my step-brother Gilla said immediately.

Niall nodded. 'You are, but you are not pure-blooded Leprechaun, and while Seamus Ban is, he is the second born, so I suppose if the truth is to be told, then neither of you can claim kingship. However, I have reached a decision ...'

'What sort of decision?' I asked quietly. I was aware that my half-brother was glowering at me, his face becoming redder and redder. Gilla was two years older than me, and there was little brotherly love between us.

'I have decided to set both of you a certain task, and which ever one of you completes that task will be the new King of the Leprechauns.'

'Well, that sounds easy enough,' Gilla said. 'I'm stronger and faster then Seamus Ban, that should be no problem to me.'

Niall smiled. 'Ah, but I'm not going to give you a simple test of strength or speed: this task will require skill and cunning.' He stepped away from the figure-head and took two steps before he stopped and looked back. 'Whoever finds land, new land, fresh green land, for our people and the De Danann Lords will be the next King of the Leprechauns.'

And then he turned and walked away, leaving me and my step-brother looking at each other in amazement. Finally, Gilla walked away. 'Don't bother looking,' he said roughly. 'I will find the land. I will be King of the Leprechauns.'

In the days that followed, both Gilla and I poured over the few De Danann books and charts that had been brought along, looking for anything – a clue, a hint, a suggestion – that might at least give us some indication where new land might lie.

We found nothing.

Our charts showed the Isle of the Tuatha De Danann, and the four De Danann cities. On the edges of the map, they showed that there was some land to the far south and west, but the wind and sea had been carrying us north and east, and the other charts were blank in that direction. We spoke to the older Leprechaun sailors, but they all told the same story – there was no land to the east of the De Danann Isle.

Finally, I decided that there was nothing more I could do – the charts showed nothing, the sailors knew nothing. Maybe there was no land. Maybe we were doomed to sail on until we fell off the edge of the world. As I walked away from the charts, my step-brother laughed, knowing I had given up.

I went and stood beside the figurehead, staring out at the great banks of fog, listening to the waves slapping against the sides of the craft – and dreaming.

And that's when I spotted the bird.

For a single moment I was unsure whether it was

real, or a figment of my imagination and the fog. I thought nothing of it at first – until I suddenly realised that this was the first creature I had seen since we had left the De Danann Isle. And where there were birds, there was land ...

My excited shouts brought the whole crew running, but by the time they had gathered around, the bird had vanished back into the fog.

I pointed into the shifting wall of grey. 'There was a bird, a seabird, with a black head and black-tipped wings. It must have been heading towards land ...'

'Well there's no bird there now,' Gilla said, his eyes small and black in his red face.

'There was!' I insisted.

'Well, I don't believe it,' my step-brother said with a sneer.

Niall raised both hands. 'Tell us,' he said quietly, 'which way did it go?'

I pointed with his right hand.

'And during the time you saw it, was it moving in a straight line?'

I nodded.

Niall looked at the navigator. 'Follow that course.'

'But sire ...' the Leprechaun navigator protested, 'we could be turning in a circle ...'

'Follow it!' Niall snapped.

The metal craft swung ponderously in the grey ocean and followed the direction I had given. It held to that course for the rest of the morning. At first most of the Leprechaun crew lined the rails, anxiously peering through the grey banks of fog, but there were no

13

further sightings of the bird.

And no sign of land.

Around noon, when even my father was beginning to look doubtful, and Gilla's smile was becoming broader and broader, I caught a flicker of movement out of the corner of my eye. Shading my eyes with my hand, I squinted hard ... and then I pointed: a large black headed seabird had appeared out of the fog, its broad wings beating strongly.

Moments later the fog cleared and a small green island rose up out of the sea before us. The Small Folk started cheering, and our joyous cries brought the De Danann folk up on deck, and they too joined in the applause.

I was a hero. I would be the next King of the Leprechauns ... and I had discovered the island that would one day become the Land of Erin.

2

THE MASTER BUILDER

MANY STORIES ARE told about the Goban Saor, the famous wandering builder and stonemason. He was a strange mysterious creature, not fully human, but not part of the Otherworld either. Usually, he would appear in some small town with his son, build a church, a tower or even a bridge and then disappear in the night before he could be paid. He once said that a person's thanks and the joy of building was payment enough.

Some people said that he was Goibniú, the famous De Danann blacksmith, but Goibniú only worked in metal, while the Goban Saor only worked in wood and stone.

The Goban Saor could not be hired, and though many people offered him huge sums to work for them, money was unimportant and he chose what he wanted to work on.

And not everyone who approached him was human. The Devil once tried to trick him into building a bridge out of Hell, and on one occasion, the Queen of Otherworld asked him to build a palace in her fort deep beneath the ground ...

The Goban Saor never worked on Mondays. He often told his wife and son that working on Monday was a bad way to start the week. So, every Monday morning during the spring and summer months, he would get up at the first light, wake his son and together they

15

would go down to the nearby river and spend the day fishing. During the winter, when the snow lay thick outside, they would sit before the huge turf fire and the Goban Saor would tell his son about his adventures in different lands and the different buildings he had created.

Early one Monday morning in the middle of summer the Goban Saor and his son, Cathal, were just finishing their breakfast when there was a gentle knock on the door.

The Goban Saor glanced out through the half-open window: the sun was still below the horizon and the night-stars still sparkled in the purple sky. 'It's early,' he murmured, glancing across at his wife, Moire. 'I wonder who that can be?'

'Trouble,' said his wife, who had a touch of fairy blood in her and so was able to see the fairy-folk and sometimes even tell the future.

'Well if it's trouble, don't answer it,' Cathal said, looking at his parents. He lifted the carved wooden mug that his father had made for him and swallowed down the last of his milk.

There was another knock on the door and it was harder this time.

'Don't answer it,' Moire said, frowning deeply. 'It means trouble, I'm sure of it.'

'But there might be something wrong,' the Goban Saor protested, looking from his wife to the door.

The third time the knock was so loud that the door rattled in its frame.

'Well, if I don't answer the knock, it's a new door

we'll be needing, because the next knock is sure to take it off its hinges,' the Goban Saor said, pushing his chair away from the table and stamping over to the door. He was a short, bald, broad man, with a wide face and his eyes were the colour of the sea on a summer's day. His hands were huge and it was commonly believed that he was the strongest man in Erin.

'Who's there?' he called, leaning against the door and pressing his pointed ear against the polished wood.

There was no reply.

Cathal got up from the table and joined his father by the door. He was very like the Goban Saor, except that he was a little taller, his hair was a deep brown and his eyes, like his mother's, were green. And although he was only ten years, he was already stronger then most fully grown men. He lifted the heavy stonemason's hammer from the toolbox by the door.

'Who's there?' the Goban Saor called again, but at the same time he quickly flung open the door and dashed outside. Cathal ran after him into the misty morning.

There was no one outside.

The Goban Saor looked troubled. He threw back his head and breathed in the chill morning air. He could smell the damp dew, the rich earth and the distant salt of the sea. He could even smell the odour of rabbits in their burrow nearby and the mustiness of wet feathers and straw from a sparrow's nest in the trees above. But he could smell no other odours; no smell of men or beasts. Kneeling on the ground, he examined the doorstep for any sign of footprints, but there were none.

Cathal tapped his father on the shoulder and he stood up, and silently pointed to the door-knocker which was battered and twisted out of shape.

The Goban Saor ran his fingers across the twisted metal.

'Who could have done this?' Cathal whispered, looking at the door-knocker in amazement. His father had made the knocker from a piece of curiously shaped metallic stone Cathal had seen falling from the sky. It had taken all of the Goban Saor's great strength and skill to shape the incredibly strong stone. 'It would have taken great strength to do this sort of damage,' Cathal said.

'I don't like it,' the Goban Saor said, looking back over his broad shoulder at the neat little garden. 'It looks like fairy-work to me.' He turned back to his son. 'I don't think we'll be going fishing today,' he added.

'But who was knocking on the door – and where did they go?' Cathal asked, as he followed his father back inside. And then they were both stopped in astonishment, for sitting calmly at the table were two strangers.

They were tall, thin men, with pale faces and slightly slanting eyes the colour of wet grass. They were wearing long green cloaks of shimmering metallic material and two silver helmets rested on the table beside them.

Moire looked up as her husband and son came in. Her face was expressionless as she nodded at the two strangers. '*Sidhe*-folk,' she said calmly. 'I told you it

18

would be trouble,' she added.

The two strangers stood up, their cloaks opening a little to reveal that they were wearing beautiful silver armour over chain-mail. Each one also wore a jewelled sword and a knife on their belts. They both bowed slightly. They were so alike that they might have been twins.

'You are the Goban Saor?' one of them asked.

The stonemason nodded. 'I am the Goban Saor – but before you start, I don't work on Mondays and I certainly don't like to see strangers come uninvited into my home.'

'And you damaged the knocker,' Cathal added.

The knight standing before him bowed slightly. 'I am sorry. I sometimes forget that the *Sidhe*-folk are far stronger than humans. We will see that it is repaired.'

'I do my own work,' the Goban Saor said quickly. 'Now what do you want?' he demanded.

'We have a task for you,' one of the *Sidhe*-knights said quickly.

'I told you, I don't work on Mondays, and I'm not sure I want to work for the *Sidhe* anyway.'

One of the knights stepped forward, and now that he was close, Cathal could see tiny differences between him and the second *Sidhe*. He smiled, showing shining pointed white teeth. 'I am Net,' he said, 'Chief advisor to Maeve, Queen of the *Sidhe*. This is my son Ronan. I have been sent here by the queen,' he continued, 'because she wishes you to build her a palace.' He paused, then said, 'Think about that: the opportunity to design and build a palace for the Queen of the Otherworld.'

'What sort of palace?' the Goban Saor asked, beginning to get interested now.

'The design is up to you. All our queen demands is that it will be the most beautiful palace either in your world or in ours. You will have all the building materials you need. We can make gold or silver, diamonds or emeralds or, indeed, any sort of precious metal or stone for you to use. But the palace must be magnificent ...'

'Everything my father builds is magnificent,' Cathal said quickly.

'That is true,' the Goban Saor said with a smile.

'Well, can you do it?' Ronan, the younger *Sidhe* asked, but his father shook his head slightly.

'You must not ask the Goban Saor that,' he said. 'Of course he can do it – *only* he can do it.'

The Goban Saor nodded, 'I could ... if I wanted to.'

'You would be well rewarded,' Ronan began, but Net silenced him with a quick angry look.

'This is the Goban Saor – he cannot be bought.' Net looked at the stonemason and smiled slightly, showing his teeth again. 'But I think the Goban Saor will do it, if only for the challenge.'

The Goban Saor considered, running his huge hands across his bald head. He *would* like to create the fairy palace: it would be the most exciting building he had ever made ... and to be able to work with any sort of stone or metal would be almost like a dream come true.

He looked around at his son, and raised his eyebrows slightly. 'Well, what do you think?' he asked softly.

'It would be nice to build a fairy palace,' Cathal said, 'but can you trust these two, or their queen?'

The Goban Saor then looked over at his wife. 'What do you think?' he asked.

Moire smiled at her husband. She already knew that he had made up his mind to do it. She wiped her hands in her apron. 'I think you should be very careful,' was all she would say.

The Goban Saor turned back to the two fairy-folk. 'I'll do it,' he said.

Net bowed again. 'I knew you would,' he said. 'Now, when the job is finished, you will receive as your payment a house full of gold ...'

The Goban Saor said nothing.

'Two houses full of gold,' Net said.

The Goban Saor shrugged and stuck his hands in his pockets.

'Two houses full of gold and one house full of jewels,' the *Sidhe*-knight said.

The Goban Saor looked up. 'I don't want fairy-gold,' he said suddenly. 'A friend of mine found some fairy gold which turned to dust when the *Sidhe* grew angry with him. No, I want a field full of cows, another of sheep, a prize bull, a ram and some pigs and hens. And,' he added, 'I want them to be real creatures, not fairy-beasts.'

Net frowned. 'I don't understand,' he said softly. 'We are offering you riches beyond your wildest dreams and you ask for farm animals?'

'What would I do with all that wealth?' the Goban

21

Saor asked. 'No, give me the animals – I'll be satisfied with them. You can tell me tomorrow morning before we go if you will give me what I want.'

'But you must leave now,' Ronan said quickly.

The Goban Saor smiled and shook his head.

'This is Monday,' Cathal said with a grin. 'My father never works on a Monday.'

THE FOLLOWING MORNING the sky hadn't even begun to pale in the east by the time the Goban Saor and Cathal were finished breakfast. They were just gathering up their tools when there was a knock on the door, a gloved fist pounding on the wood.

'It's open,' the Goban Saor called out, turning to face the door.

The door opened and Net stepped in. He was dressed much as he had been the previous day, but now his long dark-green cloak was speckled with tiny drops of water that sparkled like silver beads on the cloth. Wisps of chill grey fog drifted in through the open door.

'It is time,' the *Sidhe*-knight said softly, bowing to the Goban Saor.

'Have we far to go?' Cathal asked.

'I have brought mounts for you both,' Net said turning away.

'We'll be with you shortly,' the Goban Saor called after him. He turned back to Moire, his wife. 'Now, remember what I told you,' he said mysteriously, and then kissed her on the cheek, gathered up his tools and walked out into the cold, damp morning.

Cathal kissed his mother. 'We'll be home soon,' he whispered, and then ran out after his father.

There were a dozen fairy-folk waiting outside in the garden. They were sitting silently on their strange fairy-steeds, tall, thin animals, with flat, cat-like eyes. The *Sidhe* were muffled up in their dark cloaks, with metal helmets on their heads, and they were all carrying tall metal spears. Cathal stepped closer to his father; with the fog swirling and twisting about them they looked sinister and frightening.

But the Goban Saor was without fear. He squeezed Cathal's shoulder gently and turned to Net. 'Where's my horse – and it'd better not be one of these underfed nags,' he added with a laugh.

The *Sidhe* lord smiled and said something in the fairy-folk's own language and then Ronan came out of the mist leading a red bull that was taller then he was. It was a huge, broad creature, with fantastically curling horns, but its eyes, like those of the horses, were like a cat's.

'I can't ride that,' the Goban Saor said.

'This is Borua, the Red Bull, and it's the only creature we could find that'd carry your weight.'

'What about me?' Cathal asked

'You can ride one of our own horses,' Ronan said. 'But your father is so heavy he would have crushed them.'

'But a bull!' the Goban Saor said. He shook his head in amazement and laughed. 'Come on then,' he said to his son. 'Let's get going.'

His father held the reins while Cathal mounted one

of the fairy-steeds, and even though he was still only a boy, the beast groaned beneath his weight.

The Goban Soar then climbed up on to the broad back of the red bull. Borua turned its heavy head and stared at the man on its back, steam snorting from its nostrils. The Goban Saor stared at it, almost as if he was daring it to do something, and finally the beast looked away. Net climbed up onto his own horse, bowed to Moire who was standing in the doorway, watching them, and then he turned away. He had taken perhaps ten steps when he disappeared into the twisting, shifting grey mist. Without a word, and only the tiniest of sounds, the rest of the fairy-folk followed in a line behind him. When the last horse, with Cathal on its back, had trotted into the mist and vanished from sight, the bull took a few steps forward after it. The Goban Saor turned and waved at his wife, until he too was swallowed up by the grey dampness.

Moire waited until even the sounds of the riders had disappeared before she turned back and closed the door gently behind her. She wondered when she would see her husband and son again. She also wondered *if* she would ever see her husband and son again.

BEFORE THE SUN rose high in the heavens and the mist still lingered, the Goban Saor realised that the fog was unnatural. It could only have been made by the fairy-folk.

He glanced over at his son riding alongside him. Cathal was looking up in to the sky where the sun was now just a pale orange glow. Cathal leaned across his fairy-horse to whisper urgently to his father. 'What's happening, where are we? And why doesn't this fog lift?' His hair was plastered to his head with the damp fog and he was chilled right through to the bone.

'The fairy-folk are creatures of twilight, they cannot stand the sunlight,' his father said. 'They have lived so long underground now, that the sun burns their pale skin and hurts their eyes. Their magicians have created this mist to protect them until we reach their fort and go beneath the earth.'

'Have we much further to go?' Cathal wondered.

The Goban Saor shook his head. 'I shouldn't think so. It would take a great power to keep this magical mist about us for a long time. If we had a long way to go, they would have come for us during the night. No,' he shook his head, 'I think we're going to that fairy-fort just up along the coast, not far from the Cliffs of Moher.'

Cathal nodded quickly. 'I know it, that low green mound in the field that belongs to the Dillane Family.'

His father smiled. 'That's the one: it's the nearest fairy-fort to us. And if that's where we're going then I think we should be there very soon ...'

He had hardly finished talking when Net and Ronan appeared out of the mist. They were both smiling. 'We have arrived,' Net said. They rode forward a few more paces and the fog thinned out and they found that they were facing one of the low grassy mounds which the country people called a fairy-fort.

Net dismounted and walked to the edge of the

mound, just where the ground began to rise. He stamped down hard on the earth and said something in the fairy speech, which sounded rather like Old Irish, but not quite.

And slowly ... slowly ... slowly ... slowly, a huge doorway appeared in the grassy mound. The doors were tall and golden, divided into four panels set into the metal, and each panel was deeply etched with an ancient Celtic design.

The Goban Saor looked at the doors carefully, and then he nodded. 'Good workmanship that.'

Net smiled thinly. 'It should be. They were design-ed by Credenus, the Craftsman for the Tuatha De Danann, and created by Giobniú and his apprentice, Daire.' The *Sidhe* Lord then spoke again in his strange, almost-familiar language, and the doors opened very slowly. Cathal almost expected them to creak as they opened, but they were silent.

Behind the doors there was nothing but darkness.

Net took a few steps forward, until he was almost at the edge of the opening. He raised both hands high and said something in the fairy-language, and imme-diately a deep blue-green glow lit up the tunnel. The fairy-lord lowered his hands. 'This is the way to the Otherworld,' he said, stepping through. The fairy-host followed him silently.

The Goban Saor and Cathal each took a deep breath and then followed the *Sidhe* into the opening. Once they were inside the mound, Net turned back and clapped his hands. For an instant nothing happened and then the two massive doors swung silently closed.

26

Now there was no turning back.

The Goban Saor and Cathal followed the host down the long, long corridor for what seemed like hours, but which the Goban Saor decided couldn't have been more then twenty minutes. Soon the rock walls of the fort changed from rough stone into polished marble and carved into the marble were scenes from the *Sidhe*'s history.

As they rode past Cathal looked in wonder and listened as his father told him the stories that were carved into the walls ...

Here was a ship carrying the first of the Tuatha De Danann to Erin ... and here was another carving showing their battles with the Fir Bolg and the Formorians, two tribes of terrible demons who ruled Erin before them. Another stretch of wall showed how Nuada, King of the De Danann, lost his mind, and then it showed Diancecht, the Physician, making him a hand of shining silver that was just as good as his own hand, and from then on he was known as Nuada of the Silver Hand. On the other side of the wall, a carving showed the second Battle of Mag Turiadh. Here was Lugh of the Long Arm killing the demon-king Balor who only had one eye ... but the eye had power to turn a man to dust simply by looking at him.

As they neared the end of the tunnel, the last section of wall showed the De Danann leaving the world and going into their Secret Places, the fairy-forts, or their palaces under lakes or mountains, or moving to some of the islands that sometimes appeared and then swiftly disappeared off the west coast of Erin.

The fairy host suddenly stopped. Cathal, who had been looking at the walls, turned around and found that they had reached a second set of doors. These doors, unlike the first set, were plain, and had been carved from warm yellow metal. He looked over at his father. 'Is that what I think it is?' he asked, nodding towards the doors.

The Goban Saor nodded. 'It's gold all right.'

Net placed both hands on the right-hand door, and his son placed his hands on the left-hand side. They pushed together – and the doors swung open. The fairy-host quickly trotted their horses inside, and for the first time that day, they began to chat and laugh together, pulling off their silver helmets, running their long-fingered hands through fine pale hair. Soon, only Net and his son and the Goban Saor and Cathal remained outside.

'This is the Land of Fairy,' Net said proudly. 'You are honoured: very few humans have ever passed beyond these gates.'

'And even fewer have ever come back,' the Goban Saor said with a smile.

Net's smile faded. 'Of course, you will be allowed to leave – once your task is finished.'

'Of course we will,' the mason said, looking at his son. 'Well, shall we go in?' he asked, urging Borua forward.

Net and Ronan stood aside and allowed the mason and his son to enter the Fairy Land. Once they had passed through the golden doors, the *Sidhe* lords pushed them closed behind them, but the Goban Saor and his son didn't notice. They both sat on their strange mounts with their mouths open in amazement.

There was a sky above their heads! A blue sky with clouds and birds flying slowly across it. In the distance they could see the blue line of the sea, and off to one side were mountains, some of them topped with snow. There were even houses and cottages close by, and in the distance they could see the jumbled shape of a town.

Cathal turned to the fairy-lord. 'But I thought we were inside a cave,' he said.

Ronan smiled. 'You are.'

'But the sky,' Cathal protested, 'the sea. What about all this?' he asked, swinging his arm around.

'Magic,' the fairy-lord said simply. 'You must remember that we are the greatest magicians and sorcerers in the world.'

'If you're so good at magic,' the Goban Saor asked, 'why then do you need me to make you a palace? Why don't you just conjure one up out of the ground?'

Ronan looked uncomfortable. He looked first at his father and then shrugged. 'You had better ask the queen that,' he said finally.

'I will,' the Goban Saor promised.

They rode slowly across the fairy landscape. Net led the way on his silver horse, with Cathal behind him, then the Goban Saor on the huge bull with the curling horns, followed by Ronan on his fairy-horse. They passed fields in which the fairy-folk would stop and stare blankly at the two human riders in amazement, watching them as if they were some strange alien creatures. The Goban Saor, who had seen the *Sidhe*-folk before, ignored them, but Cathal looked at them in astonishment. The people of the *Sidhe* were mostly tall and thin, with long, pointed faces, slanting eyes and pointed ears. But there were others who were short and stout, with a reddish colour to their skin. They had bushy hair and all the men wore beards. Then there were others who had brown skin and sharp, sharp eyes, and seemed to wear only green cloth. And once, when they were passing a river, a bald head popped up from beneath the water, and cold, fish-like eyes looked at them curiously for a few moments, before disappearing without a ripple. There were many different races in the Otherworld.

Cathal saw animals the like of which he had never seen before. He saw huge, vivid red butterflies, each one as big as a plate, spread out on some rocks by the side of the road, warming themselves. Beside them, tiny birds, no bigger then his little finger, dipped and rose among the rocks, picking insects from between the stones.

There were fairy-horses everywhere, and he saw more of the fairy-bulls, similar to the one his father was riding, although none quite so big. He also saw sheep whose fleece was of pure gold, and other whose coats seemed to be made of shining, twisted strands of glass.

At last they reached the outskirts of the town.

The Goban Saor and his son had visited most of the towns in Ireland, and had even visited the city of London, but they had never seen anything in their travels that looked like the fairy-town.

Most of the houses were long and low like the fairy-mounds; they had no windows, no chimney and only one door. The lower half of the house was covered with thousands of tiny polished stones, while the upper half of the house and the roofs were encased with gold, silver or bronze.

The main street was paved with polished black marble, while the smaller side streets were paved with white stone. It was a very lovely, but a very strange town, Cathal thought.

'Does this town of yours have a name?' the Goban Saor asked.

Net looked back and shook his head. 'There is no need: it is the only town here.'

The *Sidhe* lord led them through the town and down towards a wide stretch of water. He stopped and pointed towards the lake. 'The queen would like her palace built there.'

'On the banks of the lake?' the Goban Saor asked.

The fairy-lord shook his head. 'No: you will drain the lake and build it in the hollow that will remain.'

'That's impossible!' Cathal said, but his father held up this hand.

'It's not impossible,' he said, 'just very, very difficult.' He turned back to Net. 'I would like to meet the queen,' he said.

The fairy-lord shook his head again. 'I do not think ...' he began, but then stopped, and suddenly bowed to someone behind the stonemason and his son.

The Goban Saor and Cathal turned around and discovered a very tall, very beautiful woman standing

31

behind them. She was one of the *Sidhe*, but she was not as thin as the rest of the fairy-folk, nor was her face as pointed or sharp. She had a mane of flaming red hair that hung down to the back of her knees, and she wore a dress of red cloth trimmed with green. Around her head was a thin golden band, and there were golden bracelets on her wrists. She wore sandals of gold.

'I am Maeve,' she said simply. Her voice was soft and gentle, making it sound as if she were whispering. 'I am Queen of the *Sidhe*.'

The mason and his son bowed deeply.

'I have been waiting to meet the famous Goban Saor,' she said softly. 'I have heard a lot about you. It is said that you are the best builder in the human world.'

'That is true,' the Goban Saor said proudly. 'I am the best builder in the human world – and you'll find none better in this world either,' he added.

The queen smiled. 'I know; I've looked,' she said. 'I have a job for you, Goban Saor,' she continued. 'I want you to build me a palace – the finest in any world. It must be very special – and I want it built there!' She pointed at the lake.

The Goban Saor folded his arms across his massive chest and rocked back and forth on his heels. 'What about the water?' he asked.

The queen raised a hand and a small woman hurried up. She looked no bigger than a ten year-old girl, except that she had two horns growing out of her head. The queen pointed towards the lake. 'Take away the water,' she said.

The small woman trotted out to the water's edge

and raised both hands high. She then tilted her head back and began to chant aloud in a strange high-pitched language. The air went suddenly cold and there was a sharp, bitter smell.

The Goban Saor and his son watched in silence as a small white cloud began to twist and curl around, and as it did, it began to darken in colour. The small woman stopped and clapped her hands together three times, and then, first in drops and then in a solid stream, the water of the lake poured upwards into the cloud.

In a few minutes the lake was gone and in its place was a deep round hole in the ground. The cloud, which was now dark and heavy-looking, began to drift away, but the small woman stopped it with a word, and then looked at the queen.

'Where?' was all she said, in a strange, thick accent.

'To the sea,' the queen said.

The small woman turned and pointed towards the distant blue line of the sea. 'Go,' she said. The cloud obediently drifted away towards the sea.

Maeve turned back to the Goban Saor. 'The water is gone.'

The mason nodded. 'Yes, I can see that – but there is one thing you must tell me first.

'You have only to ask,' the queen said.

'You have great magical powers,' the Goban Saor said. 'I have just seen your sorceress do something I would have thought impossible – even for one of the Tuatha De Danann. Now tell me, if you have so much power, why can you not use your own magic to create a palace?'

The queen didn't answer immediately. She slowly looked around at the empty lake, the town, and the blue sky with its white, fluffy clouds before turning back to the stonemason. 'You see all this,' she said. 'This is all an illusion.'

'An illusion?' Cathal asked.

Maeve nodded. 'Yes, an illusion is something you see which is not really there.'

'So there is no sky, no clouds, no grass ...?' Cathal asked.

But the queen shook her head. 'The grass, the bushes, the trees and the animals are real, for they were created by the first of the De Danann folk to come into the Secret Places when their magic was strong. But the sky and clouds are illusion; above our heads there is only the cold grey stone.'

'But what about the lake?' Cathal wondered. 'That was no illusion – was it?' he asked.

Maeve smiled. 'No, that was no illusion; and it was no great feat of magic. All that happened then was that the water was shifted from one place to another.'

'So, you couldn't really build a palace,' the Goban Soar said. 'All you could make would be an image, a picture.'

Queen Maeve nodded.

The Goban Saor walked over to where the lake had been and looked down into the hollow. He rubbed his two large hands together. 'Well, when do we start?' he asked.

'Now!' the queen said.

THE GOBAN SAOR and his son worked for over a year on the fairy-palace. The queen gave them everything they wanted, and as many men as they needed. The fairy palace rose quickly.

The Goban Saor was using blocks of bronze for the building, but every now and again he would add a block of silver, just for effect. He gave it four tall thin towers, also of bronze, topped with pointed roofs of silver, and he put in a lot of tall, pointed windows. The roof was made of solid silver tiles, but this time with a bronze tile added every now and again just for effect. It was indeed the most beautiful palace ever built.

Soon, all that needed to be hung were the doors.

Queen Maeve came to see the Goban Saor.

'When will the work be finished?' she asked.

The huge mason rubbed his hands on his leather apron. 'Soon,' he said.

'You will tell me the moment the work is finished,' she said, turning away.

'Oh, I will,' the Goban Saor promised. He stood watching while the queen got into her black and silver chariot and drove away and then he called his son. They walked around the palace pretending to examine different parts of it.

'What's wrong, father?' Cathal asked. He knew from his father's expression that something was not quite right.

The Goban Saor shook his head. 'I'm not sure,' he said, 'but I don't think that the queen will let us go when this job is finished.'

Cathal nodded slowly, but said nothing. He had

35

always thought that the queen would try to keep them in the Otherworld.

'She was here a little while ago asking when the job would be finished, and yesterday Net was here asking the same question.'

'Do you remember that lovely little bridge we built for that King of Scotland?' Cathal asked his father. 'Do you remember that he didn't want to let us go? He was going to kill us so that we would never be able to build another bridge like his ...'

The Goban Saor laughed aloud. He put his arm around his son's shoulder. 'You're a clever lad, Cathal. That's exactly what I'm thinking. This queen will have us killed the moment the job is finished,' he said.

'But how are we going to escape?'

The Goban Saor winked. 'I've got a plan,' he said.

Every day for the next week either Net, his son Ronan or the queen herself would come and see if the palace was finished. But every day either the Goban Saor or Cathal would make up some excuse, or say that they were still short of some bricks, or wood, or nails.

But time was running out and the *Sidhe* were becoming impatient.

Finally, one Saturday morning when the queen came to see what was happening, the Goban Saor said that the only thing keeping him from completing the palace was a tool he had left back home.

'Tell me what it is, and I'll have one of my men go and bring it here,' Maeve said immediately.

The Goban Saor shook his head. 'Oh. I'm afraid that I couldn't do that. This is a very special tool; in-

36

deed, it's a magical tool that was given to me by the King of Scotland as payment for a bridge I built him.'

Queen Maeve nodded. 'I have heard of the King of Scotland's bridge.'

'Well, this tool can only be handled by either my son or myself, or a member of a royal family. If anyone else touches it, it will melt.' He shrugged his shoulder. 'As soon as I have that, we'll be able to hang the doors and we'll be finished.'

The queen thought for a moment. 'Would my son be able to hold this special tool?' she said at last.

'Well he is a prince of the *Sidhe*, I'm sure that he would,' the Goban Saor said.

'Then I'll send him,' Maeve said. 'What shall he ask for?'

'Tell him to ask my wife for the long straight tool with the curly bit at the end,' he said. 'She will know what he means.'

'I will send him today,' Queen Maeve said.

SHORTLY AFTER THE sun had gone down, there was a knock on the door of the Goban Saor's house. Moire put down her knitting and opened the door to find a young red-haired boy, with the sharp features of the fairy-folk, standing on the doorstep.

'You are the Goban Saor's wife?' he asked immediately in a high-pitched squeaky voice.

Moire nodded. 'I am. Who are you?'

The boy bowed slightly. 'I am Ruadh, Prince of the *Sidhe*, son of Maeve, Queen of the *Sidhe*,' he said grandly.

'And what can I do for you, Ruadh, Prince of the *Sidhe*, son of Maeve, Queen of the *Sidhe*?' Moire asked with a smile.

'I have come to fetch a tool so that your husband can finish my mother's palace,' he said.

Moire smiled again, and her smile was wider this time. 'Ah, I wondered when someone would be coming to look for that tool,' she said.

'It's a long straight tool with a curly bit at the end,' he said.

Moire nodded. 'I know the one.' She crossed the room, and pulled up the door that led down into the cellar. 'It's down here,' she said, 'But you will have to go down, because I'm afraid of the dark.'

Prince Ruadh laughed. 'We fairy-folk can see in the dark,' he said. He looked down into the cellar. 'Where's the tool?' he asked.

'Over in the corner,' Moire said.

Ruadh climbed down the wooden steps. 'I can't see it,' he shouted up – and at that moment the Goban Saor's wife dropped shut the cellar door, and pulled her chair over on top of it. She then went to the door and called out to the two guards that stood outside. 'If you wish to see your prince alive, bring my husband and son back to me by tomorrow night.'

The two *Sidhe* drew their swords and attempted to run into the house, but Moire pulled her hand out of her pocket, and held up a small golden cross. The fairy-folk stopped and took a few steps backwards with their hands up to their faces. The fairy-folk have no power against the cross.

THE TWO *SIDHE*-KNIGHTS returned to their queen and told her what had happened. When she realised that she had been tricked, she went down to the fairy palace to see the mason and his son.

'You may go now,' she said simply.

'What about my payment?' the Goban Saor asked.

'You didn't finish the job,' Maeve said 'and you won't be paid until then.'

'And if I finish the job, do you give me your word that we will be allowed to go free and be paid?' he asked.

'I give you my word,' the queen said angrily.

The Goban Saor turned around and walked over to the palace. Taking hold of one of the huge golden doors he lifted it up and held it while his son fixed it into place on its hinges. Then he did the same with the second door. He turned back to the queen. 'The job is finished.'

'So you didn't need any special tool,' she said with a touch of a smile on her thin lips.

The Goban Saor held up his two massive hands. 'These are my tools,' he said.

SO THE GOBAN SAOR tricked the fairy-folk and escaped with his life. When he returned home, he allowed Prince Ruadh to return to his own country, and then he and his wife and son lived for a long time afterwards.

No one knows what happened to the Goban Saor. Some say he and his son still wander the roads of Erin, sometimes stopping and building a small house or cottage, and then disappearing before they can be paid.

3

THE MAGICAL COWS

THERE IS AN old story told about three magical cows that came up out of the sea, and brought great riches and wealth to the land of Erin. Indeed, many rivers, lakes and wells are still called after the greatest of these magical creatures, the Bo-Fionn, the White Cow.

They were a gift from Manannan, the Lord of the Sea, but first he sent his daughter to tell the humans about these special creatures ...

It was a bright, hot summer's evening when Eila, the mermaid, swam up onto the smooth sandy beach on Erin's western shore. She pushed her way up along the warm sand and sat down with her back to a tall stone that had been nicely warmed by the day's sun. The mermaid swept her golden-green hair from her eyes and looked around. The beach was deserted, but there were fishing nets laid out to dry on the sands and lobster pots were neatly stacked in small bundles further down the beach, just beneath the tall, dark cliffs. The mermaid drew up her long, shining fish-tail and decided to wait; there was sure to be someone along soon. While she was waiting, she began to sing, and her beautiful, high, thin voice rang out in the still evening air ...

Orla heard the singing and sat up suddenly, the sound bringing her fully awake. She stood up and walked over to the edge of the cliff and peered down onto the beach, looking for the singer. But she could see no one so she walked slowly and carefully down along the cliff tops, every now and again looking back at her father's sheep which she had spent the day minding. She glanced over at the sun, which was now very low in the sky, almost touching the water, and guessed the time; another few minutes and her father and brothers would be along to bring in the sheep for the night, and she could go home then.

Suddenly the singing stopped. Orla stopped also, wondering where the sound had gone – or indeed, if it had ever been there in the first place. It had been so beautiful, so wild, so natural – in fact, it sounded almost like part of the sea. She was turning away when something caught her attention and she looked down again; there was something gleaming silver down on the beach. She was about to head back for the path that led down to the sands when she heard someone calling her name. 'Orla ... Orla ... where are you?'

'Here, here!' She stood up on her toes and waved her arms in the air, and then she saw her father's bright red hair and beard, and behind him she could make out the red hair of her two older brothers.

Cullen Mór hurried up, his long hunting spear held tightly in his hand, and he had a sword strapped across his back. There was a frown on his round brown face. 'Where have you been?' he demanded. 'I thought I told you to mind the sheep.'

'I have been minding the sheep,' Orla protested, 'but I heard a sound down on the beach ...'

'What sort of sound?' her father asked quickly. 'Voices? Boats?' He walked past her and peered down onto the beach which was already falling into shadow. There had been some pirate raids further down along the coast over the past few months and while they hadn't come this far north yet, he was still worried.

Orla shook her head, her copper-red hair shining orange and gold in the sunset. 'No, not that sort of sound.'

'Well what sort of sound?' her father snapped.

'A sort of singing.'

'Singing?'

Orla nodded. 'Singing,' she said.

'It was probably just the waves rushing through the caves down in the cliffs,' Cullen, her eldest brother said, coming up behind his father.

But Orla shook her head. 'No it was someone singing – and it was down there.' She turned around and pointed to where she had seen the spot of silver on the beach. But the light was almost gone now and she couldn't see anything. 'Oh,' she said, 'well it was there.'

'Aye,' Cullen Mór said, not sure whether he believed her. Although he loved his daughter dearly, he knew that she sometimes made up little stories. He looked back over his shoulder to where Ross, his younger son, was rounding up the sheep. 'Well, no harm done, eh? Let's go home then.'

And down on the beach Eila heard the voices in the

42

distance and began to sing again, hoping to attract their attention.

Orla squealed with surprise when she heard the wild and beautiful voice singing again. 'That's it, that's it, that's it,' she cried happily.

'Aye, but what is it?' her father asked, pulling his sword free, wondering whether it was a trap.

Cullen swung his bow off his shoulder and pulled an arrow from his belt. He looked at his father. 'What should we do?' he asked.

'Get your brother first. Did he bring his bow also?' He hurried on when Cullen nodded. 'You and I will creep down onto the beach while he stays up here just in case we're attacked. If it is a trap he can fire down onto them and allow us to escape. Right, off you go then.'

'What about me?' Orla asked.

Her father considered for a few moments. 'Well, I can't send you home alone now that the sun has just about gone down, so you will stay up here with your brother. And don't get in his way. If anything happens down there, we'll need him to protect us.'

'But what could possibly attack you?' Orla asked. 'That sounds like a woman's voice. But, oh, it's so beautiful.'

Her father looked worried. 'Aye, that it is; perhaps just a little too beautiful. Let's hope it's not a banshee, eh?'

'A fairy woman?' Orla whispered, beginning to get a little frightened now. She had often heard about the terrible banshee, the fairy woman who would come

43

and sing outside someone's house, warning them that there would soon be a death in the family.

Ross came running up then with Cullen. Although there was nearly two years between the two boys, they looked almost identical, because Ross, although the younger, was now the same height as his brother, and had the same bright red hair and green eyes. He was grinning widely as he knelt down on the cliff top and fitted an arrow to his bow.

'What's so funny?' Orla asked.

Ross turned to look at her and winked. 'I haven't had so much fun for weeks,' he said. 'Mysterious voices down on the beach; father and Cullen going down to investigate, swords, spears and bows and arrows at the ready, and me up here to shoot down at anything that attacks them. Why, it's the sort of thing stories are made of.'

Orla smiled too. Soon her brother would be going off to train as a bard; he loved all the old stories and tales and was always telling them to her. His biggest complaint was that nothing exciting ever happened now. Suddenly she touched his arm. 'Listen!'

Ross shook his head. 'I can't hear anything,' he said.

His sister nodded. 'The singing's stopped,' she whispered.

Ross peered over the cliff edge and looked down onto the beach. He could just about make out the shapes of his father and brother as they crept along the sands, running from boulder to boulder, making their way towards the spot where the sounds had come from.

'Did you see anything down there?' he asked his sister.

Orla nodded, and then pointed out to the water's edge. 'I thought I saw something shining silver there,' she said.

Ross pulled back his arm, and the bow creaked a little in his hands. It was a good distance away, but he thought he could hit anything or anyone that might be hiding down there.

Suddenly, they both heard a voice drifting up from the beach. A thin, high, very beautiful woman's voice.

'You have nothing to fear from me.'

Down on the beach, both Cullen and his father dived for the ground when the voice spoke. They lay on the damp sand wondering what they were going to do next, when they heard the speaker laughing.

'I told you, you really have nothing to fear from me. I'm not going to harm you -- and I am alone, I promise.'

'Who are you?' Cullen asked, while his father began to creep around behind the woman whom they still couldn't see.

'My name is Eila,' the woman said.

'What are you doing on our beach?'

'Your beach?' Eila said. 'When did this become your beach?' she asked, a touch of anger in her voice now.

'Our farm is up yonder, beyond the cliffs. This beach is part of our property.'

'This beach – and all the seashores of Erin – are the

property of the Lord of the Sea, and the Sea-Folk.'

'And who is this Lord of the Sea?' Cullen asked, trying to keep the woman's attention on him. He could see that his father was almost up beside the rock behind which the woman was hiding.

'Manannan is the Lord of the Sea,' Eila said proudly. 'He is my father.' She suddenly screamed as a man darted around the rock with a long spear in his hand. He stopped, shocked to find a woman with a fish-tail instead of feet and shouted in surprise. Eila leaned back against the stone and swept upwards with her long tail, knocking the spear from the man's hands, sending him falling backwards with fright. Eila then dived for the sea – and there was a thin buzzing sound and something long and hard zipped into the sand by her outstretched arm. Another whizzed into the sand by her tail, and a third cracked against the stone, shattering into two.

'Stay where you are,' a voice called from the distance.

Cullen came running up, his bow ready, pointing at the mermaid. He helped his father up. 'Are you all right?'

'Aye,' Cullen Mór nodded. 'It was more of a fright that she gave me than anything else. I got a shock when I saw that tail, and then she hit me with it, and I fell on the sand. I'm all right. You'd better tell your brother and sister to come down.'

Cullen looked at the mermaid and then back to his father. 'Are you sure you'll be all right? I mean she might be a sorceress, and work some of the spells on you while I'm away.'

'The Sea-Folk can only use their magical powers in water,' Eila said suddenly. 'We draw our power from the sea, the same way as one of your magicians would draw his power from the land.'

Cullen still looked doubtful, but his father said, 'I've heard that too. Go and fetch your brother and sister, before he puts an arrow through one of us.'

When his son had crunched off up the beach, Cullen Mór turned back to the mermaid. 'I'm sorry for all the ...' He stopped; he couldn't think of the correct word, so he just shrugged. After all, what do you say to the first mermaid you've ever met just after you've tried to kill her?

Eila smiled. 'I thought that if I just sat here quietly, someone would just happen along and I would be able to speak without frightening the life out of them. I'm the one who should be sorry. My name, by the way, is Eila, Princess of the Waves, daughter of Manannan, Lord of the Sea.'

'I am Cullen Mór,' he said. 'That was my son, who is also called Cullen; the one who was up on the cliff shooting down at you is Ross and my daughter Orla is there also. She was the first to hear you. But what are you doing here?' he asked.

The mermaid shrugged. 'My father sent me with a message,' she said.

'What sort of message?' Cullen Mór asked.

Eila hesitated. 'Well, my father said that I was only to tell it to a lord of the land, because it was important that the king got to hear of it.'

47

Cullen Mór smiled. 'I am lord of most of the west coast of Erin. If you have a message you wish to have passed on to the king, I will make sure he gets it. In fact, I'll even send my son Cullen to deliver it.'

The mermaid smiled and nodded. 'Then I will tell you ...' She stopped then as Cullen returned with his brother and sister.

Cullen Mór nodded to Ross. 'That was very good shooting,' he said.

His son smiled shyly. 'I've been practising,' he said.

'This is Eila, Princess of the Waves, daughter of the Lord of the Sea,' Cullen Mór said, introducing the mermaid. 'She has an important message from her father for the king. She was just about to tell me when you arrived.' He looked back to the mermaid.

Eila nodded. 'Well, my father has always loved the land of Erin, and he has watched over it in many little ways ever since he made his home beneath the Isle of Mona off the east coast of this land. And now, to show his great love for this country, he is going to send three of his magical cows ashore ... '

'Cows?' Cullen Mór said.

'Magical cows?' Ross asked.

Eila nodded. 'Aye; one cow alone can produce enough milk in a single morning to feed a thousand men. Each cow will give birth to a hundred fine cattle every year, and each of these in turn, will also give fine milk and produce many calves. These magical cows will never sicken, and will never die.'

Cullen Mór had become more and more excited as the mermaid told them about the cows. At that time, a man's wealth was measured by many things, by the size of his fort, by the workmanship on his jewellery, by his weapons, by the number of people who were either his servants or who called him lord, and also by the number of his cattle. Whoever had these magical cows would be fabulously wealthy. 'And these cows are for the king?' he asked, unable to hide the envy in his voice.

But surprisingly, the mermaid shook her head. 'No; and you must take care that no one is allowed to keep one of these cattle. They must be allowed to roam free at all times – otherwise, who knows what might happen? Let the animals wander where they wish; if they want to stay with any particular herd of cattle, then let them. And that is what you must tell the king. He must give a royal command that the cows are to be left alone.' Eila paused for breath and then continued. 'You see, this gift is not just for the people now, it will also bring benefits in a hundred years time.'

'How?' Orla asked in a whisper.

'Because the descendants of these cows will still be here. Erin will have the finest cattle in the world.' The mermaid looked at Cullen Mór. 'You will pass my message on to the king?' she asked.

He nodded. 'Cullen here will ride to Tara at first light and give your message to the king in person.'

Eila nodded. 'Then in exactly one month's time the three magical beasts will rise up out of the water over there.' She pointed out into the sea.

'We will be here,' Cullen Mór promised, 'and I should think the king and most of the nobles of Erin will be here also.'

'In one month's time then,' Eila said, and then she threw herself forward and splashed into the waves. For a few moments her head bobbed on the water and then with a wave of her hand, she turned and flipped down into the deep dark sea, and was gone.

THE TIME PASSED very quickly, and soon all the lords and their ladies began making their way westwards, and the tall dark cliffs sprouted brightly coloured tents like flowers. The king and queen were the last to arrive, and they rode in on the morning of the last day.

King Cormac rode in a beautifully polished leather and shining gold chariot which was pulled by two golden-brown horses. Behind him, his queen and her ladies rode in small decorated chariots. They were guarded by a hundred of the finest warriors in the land and, with the early morning sun shining on their polished armour and weapons they looked like bronze statues come to life.

The king swung his chariot around in a tight circle and came to a stop before Cullen Mór and his two sons. 'I got your message,' he said, nodding to Cullen.

Cullen Mór bowed slightly. 'I am honoured that you decided to come.'

The king smiled. 'I could hardly refuse, now could I?' he said. Cormac was a small man, with sandy coloured hair and a thin beard which matched the colour of his eyes. 'Well, where is your mermaid?' he asked.

Cullen Mór looked over his shoulder and out to sea. 'I'm not sure if the mermaid herself will be here,'

50

he said. 'She only told us about the three magical cows which her father is presenting to us.'

The king nodded without saying a word. He stood watching his men form a line along the tops of the cliffs with their spears held high. With the rising sun behind them, he thought they looked magnificent. The king turned back to Cullen Mór. 'I suppose we should go down onto the beach,' he said.

Cullen Mór nodded and led the way down to the beach along the thin, winding track. As they were crunching their way out towards the waves, the king spoke, almost to himself.

'I wonder why Manannan is sending the cows ashore here on the west coast, when he himself lives beneath the Isle of Mona which if off the east coast.'

Cullen Mór nodded. 'That puzzled me too, but my son Ross thinks he might know the answer.' He turned and looked at his younger son.

Cormac glanced across at the young man. 'Well?' he said, 'what do you think?'

Ross gave a little cough. 'Well,' he said, '*Tír na nÓg*, the Land of Youth, lies off this coast. Perhaps the Lord of the Sea is taking the magical cows from that land.'

The king thought about it for a few moments and then he nodded, 'Yes, perhaps you are right. Do you know much about these things?' he asked then.

Ross nodded. 'I'm going to be a bard,' he said proudly.

Cormac nodded again. 'When you are a fully train-ed bard, you must come to my court.'

'I will,' Ross promised. He was about to say more

when he noticed a disturbance out at sea. He pointed. 'Look!'

In the distance they could see that the pale blue water was bubbling and frothing. Long streamers of white water shot upwards and there was a low hissing, sizzling noise. Suddenly the water shot up in a huge fountain that broke when it touched the sky and then fell down again in two beautiful half circles. A dozen small rainbows immediately formed in the dancing waters and sparkled across the early morning sky.

The fountain lasted for a few minutes and then it slowly died down and the water grew still again. Then, just when the people were beginning the think that is was all over, hundreds of tiny bubbles began to break on the surface of the water with little popping sounds. And then a larger bubble began to form. It grew bigger and bigger, changing colour all the time, from a bright blue to a pale white. It grew and grew until it was a huge milk-white ball, and then it slowly began to roll across the waves in towards the beach.

The king, Cullen Mór and his sons backed away quickly, moving further and further up the beach. The soldiers on the cliff-tops tightened their grip on their spears, ready to attack the huge bubble if it came too close to their king.

The huge white bubble continued rolling silently in towards the shore, and then an extra-large wave came up behind it and pushed it up onto the beach. The bubble bounced up onto the sand and rolled across the stones – and then it burst, with a wet pop and a hiss, splashing everyone on the beach and along the top of the cliffs with warm salty water. People immediately began rubbing their stinging eyes – and when they looked again, they found three large cows standing patiently on the wet sands.

The animals were very much like ordinary cows, except that they were a little larger, their heads a little bigger, their legs a little thinner. One was completely white, another completely black and the third was a dull red colour.

Everyone was staring at them in amazement, when a golden-green head popped up out of the water offshore, and a thin brown arm waved in the air. It was Eila.

'These are the three magical animals that my father is giving as a gift to the people of the land of Erin. They are the Bo-Fionn,' she said pointing to the white cow, 'the Bo-Dubh,' pointing to the black, 'and the Bo-Ruadh,' she pointed to the red coloured animal. 'And remember,' she warned them, 'they must be allowed to roam free always and they must never be taken by any man for his use only.' The mermaid waved again and then she disappeared back into the waves with a flip of her tail.

The three cows wandered slowly up the beach and then along the thin pathway that led to the cliffs. They looked at Cormac and Cullen Mór and his sons as they passed, but they didn't stop. When they reached the cliff top, they continued on down the track heading for the road. One of the king's men stepped into their path to try and stop them, but the animals just kept walking straight on and ignored him, and when he stepped right in front of a cow, it just butted him aside with its large head.

'Let them go ... and don't touch them,' the king ordered.

The cows continued walking down the track, with the king and his followers walking along behind them, wondering what they were going to do. However, once they reached the road, the cows turned and headed for the crossroads and there they stopped.

Everyone stopped a little way away from them.

'I wonder what they're going to do?' Cullen Mór said, almost to himself.

'They will probably split up,' Ross said. 'One of them will go north, one south and the third will probably continue straight on towards the east coast.'

'But why should they do that?' King Cormac was asking just as the three cows chose three different roads, and headed off, the red cow towards the north, the black cow to the south and the white cow taking the road that led to the east. And although they didn't seem to be walking any faster than they had before, they were quickly out of sight.

'Follow them! Follow them!' the king shouted to his men, 'but don't touch them, and don't interfere with them no matter what happens.'

Men ran to their horses and soon a dozen men had galloped off along the north and south roads after the cows.

'What about the Bo-Fionn, the white cow?' Cullen Mór asked the king.

Cormac smiled. 'I'll go after her myself. I wouldn't

54

be at all surprised if she's heading for Tara.' The king smiled so strangely that Cullen Mór was troubled.

'And if she isn't? ' he asked.

The king looked surprised. 'But the best grazing land in all Erin is around Tara. Of course she's heading there.' He paused and added greedily, 'And it is only right that any magical animals should be close to the king.'

'Remember what the mermaid said,' Ross reminded the king. 'She said the cows must not belong to any man. They must be allowed to wander where they will.'

'I heard her,' Cormac said angrily.

'Then remember it,' Cullen Mór said coldly. He turned to his sons then. 'Come, we have work to do.' And, before the king could say another word, the three men walked away leaving him standing alone on the cliff top. Cormac stared after them for a few minutes, and then he turned and looked in the direction the white cow had gone, and he smiled once again.

FOR A FEW months afterwards all Erin was talking about the three magical cows. Wherever they stopped, little rivers and wells of fresh water would spring up, and small lakes would form. And no matter where they spent the night, even if it was a rocky hillside, it would suddenly sprout rich green grass. Every morning and evening the cows would be milked and there was always more milk than could be carried away.

And so the cows rambled on. The Bo-Ruadh, which had gone into the north of the land, gave birth to two fine calves, and then she strangely disappeared, although the calves bred with ordinary animals and produced fine calves in turn. The Bo-Dubh, who had headed off into the south, also had two calves and the last that was seen of her was the tip of her tail disappearing down beneath the waves. But her calves also bred with normal cattle and they too had fine calves.

However the Bo-Fionn's tale is different. She headed off into the east at what looked like a slow and easy pace, but no matter how hard Cormac and his men tried, they didn't manage to catch up with her. She was always just the little bit ahead; always just disappearing over the top of a hill when they caught sight of her, or climbing out of a river on the other side, or reaching the other side of a bridge before them. Eventually one of Cormac's druids came to him late on the third night of the chase.

'You are wasting your time and tiring out the men and horses trying to catch this animal,' the old man said. 'This is a magical beast – and it doesn't want us to catch it.'

Cormac, who was leaning against a small tree outside his tent, turned to look at the druid. 'I wonder why that should be?' he asked with a sly smile.

'I'm wondering that too,' the druid said, and then he bowed goodnight to the king and slipped away into the darkness.

It was a similar story all across Erin. However, when they came in sight of the king's palace at Tara, what should they see in the lush green fields at the foot of the walls, but the white cow grazing contentedly!

The king clapped his hands triumphantly. 'I knew she was meant as a gift for me; why shouldn't the Lord of the Sea give a gift to the greatest king that Erin has ever seen?' he shouted.

Everyone looked a little surprised at that, because Cormac, while not being a very bad king, wasn't a particularly good one either, and he had done no brave deeds nor won any great battles.

'You will leave the cow where she is,' he said to one of his generals. 'But you will have your men build a fence from there to there.' He pointed out across the fields.

The druid, who was standing beside the king, began to speak. 'Your majesty, I must warn you ...' but the king shook his head and raised one hand.

'This animal was meant for me; the Bo-Ruadh and the Bo-Dubh can wander where they will, but the Bo-Fionn belongs to me!'

The druid shook his head. 'That is not so – and you do not realise what will happen ...' he began.

But the king just ignored the old man and rode off. The old druid watched him, shaking his head in sorrow. He wondered what would happen to the king and his court.

Nothing happened for three months. In that time the Bo-Fionn seemed quite content to wander around the huge field which the king's men had fenced in. The field bloomed, and the grass there was greener and thicker than at any other place around Tara.

And then one morning the Bo-Fionn tried to leave the field. She ambled up to the thick wooden fence and butted it with her head. The whole fence shook and wobbled. The cow hit it again and again, and then one piece of wood cracked loudly. But the noise brought Cormac's guards running up and they drove the cow away from the broken piece of wood with their spears, and kept her in the far corner of the field while carpenters repaired the break. That morning the king ordered the fence strengthened and thickened, and the carpenters worked for the next three days strengthening the wood in the fence.

Over the next few weeks the Bo-Fionn tried a few times to break out, but the king placed guards around the fence and they drove the animal back. Also the new fence was very strong, and all she succeeded in doing was to give herself a headache. And every time the cow failed to break free, she would throw back her head and moo piteously ...

... And far, far away, in the *Tír Faoi Thoinn*, the Land Beneath the Waves, Eila, princess of the waves, heard the cow's sad lowing, and she hurried to tell her father, Manannan, the Lord of the Sea.

'They won't let the Bo-Fionn go,' she said, in her strange watery language, her long tail flicking to and fro in annoyance.

Manannan sat up on his throne of polished white coral. He was a tall dark man, and looked almost human, except that his skin was a greenish colour, and his hair was also touched with green. Also, all his fingers were joined together by a thin web of flesh, like a fish.

'Why do they mock my gifts?' he demanded in his

low rumbling voice and far, far above, white waves dashed against the shores of the Isle of Mona. 'You made it clear to them that the animals were to go free at all times?' he asked his daughter.

Eila nodded. 'I told them a few times,' she said.

'Someone up there is very greedy,' the Lord of the Sea rumbled. He reached out for a huge sea-shell, and touched it with his fingertips. The inside of the shell glowed green-blue and then the colours flowed and shifted across its surface. Suddenly they steadied and Manannan and Eila found themselves looking at a picture of the Bo-Fionn trapped behind a thick and solid fence, while Cormac looked on and laughed.

The Lord of the Sea was very angry. He stamped around his palace of pearl and coral in a rage. And his anger upset the sea. Up above his watery palace, on the surface of the water, a terrible storm lashed against Mona's shores, almost completely sweeping in over the small island, and even the west coast of the Land of the Britons was washed by the frightening storm, and the east coast of Erin was also battered. But at last, Manannan thought of a plan, and this put him in such good humour that the storm above immediately died down, and the sea was as calm as a rock pool. And then all the people who lived by the sea knew that something had angered Manannan, and they wondered what he was going to do about it.

But back in the fields about Tara the Bo-Fionn was still trapped, and Cormac showed no sign that he was going to let her go. Even his beautiful wife Tuathla came to him and begged him to free the magical cow, but he still refused.

'You were not supposed to keep her,' she snapped. She was a tiny woman, with long flowing black hair and hard black eyes – and she had a terrible temper. 'Now you let that cow go this minute!'

'I will not,' Cormac shouted.

'Well if you won't – then I will!' Tuathla suddenly turned around and ran out the door, and the king could hear her heels clicking and clacking on the stone floor, disappearing into the distance.

Cormac sat on his throne and thought. Tuathla wouldn't let the cow go, would she? She was his wife, and he was the king, and he gave the orders, didn't he? And then Cormac remembered all the other times Tuathla had just laughed at his orders and did what she wanted to anyway. Suddenly he was up and running down the corridor after his wife, shouting her name.

'Tuathla, Tuathla, come back here now. Don't you dare go near that animal.' The king ran out into the courtyard, but there was no sign of his wife. He turned to a surprised looking guard. 'Where is she – which way did she go?' he demanded.

The man could only point towards the fields, and then the king was off, running as fast as he could, shouting Tuathla's name. The guard hesitated a few moments and then he too took off after the king.

By the time Cormac reached the field, Tuathla was already standing beside the Bo-Fionn with the wide gate in the fence swinging open. The queen was strok- ing the cow's large head, running her fingers down its silken coat.

'Tuathla, come out of there right now,' Cormac shouted.

'I will not,' the queen snapped and then, grabbing a handful of the cow's fleshy skin, she pulled herself up onto its broad back. She sat just behind the Bo-Fionn's head and, using her knees, she began to urge the animal towards the open gate.

The king, seeing what she was going to do, ran to the gate and began to push it closed. The guard came running up then and helped Cormac, and slowly, but surely, the heavy gate swung closed. Cormac snapped the wooden bar across it, and rubbed his hands together, smiling broadly.

'You can come out now,' he said, 'there's no escape for that animal.'

But even as he was speaking, the Bo-Fionn was beginning to trot and then to run towards the gate. Tuathla held on tightly with both hands, wondering if the cow was just going to run straight into the fence. Then the cow was galloping, almost as if it were a horse, and, just as it reached the fence, it bunched its hind legs and jumped!

The Bo-Fionn soared over the terrified king's head and landed with a solid thump on the road with Tuathla still on its back. It gave a huge bellow and galloped off down the road in a cloud of white dust.

It was never seen again.

CORMAC SENT GUARDS all over Erin looking for his wife or any trace of the white cow, but they found nothing, and *the king himself died shortly afterwards, a sorry, lonely man.*

No one knows what happened to the queen or the white cow, but many years later when Orla, the little girl who had first heard the mermaid singing, was walking along the cliff top with her own daughters, they thought they saw a huge white cow leaping and jumping among the waves with a small human woman and a mermaid on its back, laughing together.

4

THE SUNKEN TOWN

BANNOW LIES ON Ireland's south coast in the county of Wexford. It was once the site of a large mining town, but nearly all traces of the town have now gone, buried beneath the ground. All that remains now is a ruined church and some gravestones. The spot is known as the site of the Lost City of Bannow, and it is still possible to visit it ...

Donal propped his bike against the stone wall and waited for his cousins to catch up with him. They were not used to cycling and had been slowly falling behind over the last few hundred yards. He looked back; he could just see them coming up over the hill.

He leaned on the wall and stared out over the sandy hillocks towards the sea. Before him was the small overgrown graveyard and behind that the ruins of St Mary's Church. It was all that was left of what had once been the large town of Bannow.

There was a squeal of brakes behind him, and he turned around as his three cousins climbed off their bikes and flopped to the ground, red-faced and panting.

'*Wow!* You didn't tell us it was so far,' Paul, one of the boys, said.

'It's not,' Donal said, laughing. He was the oldest of

the four, having just turned twelve. He had short coal-black hair, black button eyes that always seemed to be laughing, and an Irish sense of humour. 'It can't be more than six miles.'

'Six miles!' Susan exclaimed. 'But that means another six miles back.' Susan was eleven, two years older than her twin brothers, Paul and Simon. The three cousins came from London, but were spending part of their summer holiday in the south of Ireland with their aunt and uncle. She looked up at Donal. 'That's twelve miles!' she sighed, shaking her head from side to side, her long blonde hair catching in the slight breeze.

'It's not far,' Donal said, with a smile, 'and in any case, it's worth it.'

'I hope so,' Simon said, pulling off his shoe and examining a blister on his heel. His twin, Paul, came over and showed him a blister on the palm of his hand. They were almost identical except that Simon, who was two minutes older than his brother, as he kept telling people, had slightly darker hair. Their parents often joked that Paul's hair was the colour of fresh butter while Simon's was the colour of margarine. But Donal still had trouble telling them apart.

Susan stood up. 'Well, what have you brought us here for?' she asked.

Donal pointed down towards the ruins. 'That,' he said.

'That!' Susan almost shouted. 'A graveyard and an old church. We have those back home in England,' she said.

Donal climbed up onto the wall and hopped down

into the field behind it. 'Ah, but do you have any buried towns?' he asked.

The twins looked up, suddenly interested. 'A buried town, where?'

'Down here,' Donal said. He reached up and helped Susan down into the field, while the twins scrambled up over the stone wall themselves.

'Where's the town?' Simon asked.

'Well, he did say it was buried,' Paul reminded him.

'Come on,' Donal said, 'I'll show you where it was.' He set off towards the church, with Susan beside him and the twins a little way behind. 'That's Bannow Bay,' Donal said, pointing off to the right. 'Over there is Fethard Bay, and beyond that, the Atlantic Ocean.'

Susan shaded her bright blue eyes against the glare of the sun on the water. 'What do the names mean in Irish?' she asked. During her holiday, she had become very interested in the names of places in the Irish language.

Donal thought for a few moments. 'Well, Bannow Bay could mean Piglet's Bay,' he said slowly, 'and Fethard means the High Wood, I think.'

'Piglet Bay and the High Wood Bay,' Susan repeated. She shook her head. 'I think they sound better in Irish.'

They were now in amongst the graves, quite close to the ancient church. The twins wandered amongst the old gravestones, picking bits of moss and grass off them, trying to make out the dates.

Susan pointed to the church. 'What is it called?' she

asked.

'It's called St Mary's Church,' Donal said.

'And when was it built?'

Donal shrugged. 'Some time in the thirteenth century,' he said. He pulled his jumper over his head and tied it around his waist by the sleeves. 'Come on, I'll show you the town.'

There was very little to see. There were long straight lines in the ground that marked the walls of houses and the edges of streets. Here and there stones broke through the surface of the earth, and there was a short square piece of stone stuck up from under the ground a little way, which Donal said was part of a chimney of a house buried far beneath the surface.

'What happened to the town?' Simon asked, after a while.

'The soil around here is very sandy and loose,' his cousin replied, 'and over the years the sand built up against the sides of the houses, and then began to cover them. When it began to block off the roads, the people thought it was time to leave.'

'Oh, I thought it had happened in a single night – like Atlantis,' Paul said.

'Or Pomp ... Pompeii,' Simon added.

'Oh no, this happened over a number of years, many years in fact,' Donal said. 'But in ancient times it was a very famous town, and the Danes had a mint here.'

'A mint?' Simon asked. 'What for?'

'For making coins, stupid,' his twin laughed.

'The High Street was here.' Donal said, pointing to

a long grassy rise in the ground, 'and over there was Little Street and there was Lady Street.' He turned around to Susan. 'What do you think?'

'I think I'm hungry,' she said. She looked at her small gold wristwatch. 'It's nearly half-past one.' She turned around to the twins. 'Go back to the bikes and get the food while Donal and I find some place to sit.'

'I know a good place,' her cousin said, and headed off around the side of the church.

The four cousins ate their lunch sitting on a broad, flat stone behind the old ruined church. The sun was now directly overhead and was reflected back off the old stones making all the children feel very warm and sleepy. When they were finished Donal stood up and stretched. 'Do you want to start back now?' he asked.

Susan yawned. 'In a few minutes,' she said, leaning back on the warm stone and picking an apple out of the basket. She closed her eyes and began to eat it slowly.

Donal nodded. He sat down again and rested his chin on his knees and stared out over the sparkling waters of the bay, watching the sea-birds rising and dipping slowly and then suddenly swooping into the water after some unlucky fish.

The twins wandered around the ruined church for a little while, but soon they grew too tired and came back to the warm stones to lie down and rest before the long cycle back home.

A little while later, they were all asleep.

Donal awoke first. He sat up slowly and rubbed his neck, which was stiff and sore from the position in which he had fallen asleep. He looked around. Susan stretched out on the stone beside him, fast asleep with her mouth open, snoring very daintily. A half-eaten apple lay on the ground beside her, where it was being slowly picked over by a long string of ants. The twins had fallen asleep in each other's arms in the soft bracken that grew close to the walls of the ruined church. Donal smiled; asleep they looked even more alike.

He glanced at his wrist, but then remembered that he had left his watch at home. He sat up and twisted his head to look at Susan's tiny gold watch.

Half-past four!

Donal got a fright then; they must have been asleep for over two hours. He rubbed his arms which, although they were already brown from the sun, were sore. Susan's arms, legs and face were bright red from sunburn. The twins weren't so bad because they had been sheltered by the walls of the church, but he decided he had better take them home quickly. His mother had a special cure for sunburn which she made from milk and herbs.

Donal was just about to lean over and shake Susan awake when he saw a movement out in the graveyard. It was just a flash of red and then it was gone. Donal froze, his heart beginning to beat quickly. Bannow was a lonely spot and usually when he came here there was no one around. He stayed very still.

He caught the flash of movement out of the corner of his eye again, and he had the impression of red and green and brown ... a shape – almost manlike.

68

And it was coming closer.

Susan stirred in her sleep and opened her eyes. She raised her hand to shade her face from the sun, but Donal quickly leaned over and pressed his hand over her mouth. He put his own mouth close to her ear, and whispered softly, 'Don't say a word, don't even breathe. There's something moving out in the grave-yard.'

Susan struggled to sit up, but Donal pressed her back down against the flat stone. 'Don't move,' he whispered softly. 'We're sheltered here, we can't be seen.'

The shape continued to approach the church, dodging and weaving through the gravestones, appearing for a moment and then disappearing almost into the ground. Donal squinted against the sun's glare, trying to make out the shape – although he already had an idea what it might be ...

Suddenly the figure disappeared ... and then it hopped up onto the stones directly in front of the four children!

Donal shouted with fright and Susan screamed, waking the twins. They both began to cry with fright. However, the small figure also got a fright. It balanced on the stones for a moment, its two arms waving about, then it fell off – right at Donal's feet!

It was a small, red-faced man no bigger than the twins, wearing a bright green coat and a red cap, and a pair of large silver-buckled black shoes.

'It's a cluricaun!' Donal gasped.

'A what?' Susan whispered, moving as far away

from the small man as possible.

However, once he got over his fright the cluricaun got up and dusted himself off. He then took off his cap and bowed deeply to the girl. 'He means a leprechaun, young lady,' he said in a high-pitched, almost musical voice. He then bowed deeply to the twins and finally to Donal. 'I am Donn Dearg,' he said. 'Red Donn my friends call me.'

Donal smiled with relief. He knew there was no harm in leprechauns, unless you harmed them or tried to cheat them in some way. 'My name is Donal ...' he began.

The leprechaun nodded. 'Yes, I've seen you here before,' he said.

'And these are my cousins, from London,' Donal added.

'In England,' Susan said.

'My lady,' the leprechaun said swiftly. 'I have relatives in London, England, and also in Glasgow, Scotland,' he added with a grin.

'I'm sorry, I didn't think an Irish leprechaun would know about London,' she said.

'But I belong to the Fairy Host,' the leprechaun said. 'All the leprechauns, cluricauns, fir bolg, fir dearg, banshee, Shining Ones, and the Phooka of Ireland are related to the English Hyther Spirits, Pillywiggins, Tiddy Ones, Vairies and Feeorin as well as to the Scottish Light and Dark Fairies and Elves and the ferocious Red Caps. I also have relatives in Wales among the Tylwyth Teg, the Sleigh Beggey and the Bendith y Maumau.'

When he paused for breath, Donal took the opportunity to speak. 'This is Susan, and these are the twins, Simon and Paul.'

Donn Dearg looked closely at the twins. 'In my time twins were thought to be very special people,' he said.

'We are!' Simon said quickly.

'Ah, but can you do magic, ride the wind, or raise storms or bring rain? No? But that's what I meant about being special.'

'What are you doing here?' Susan asked. 'Do you live here?'

The leprechaun suddenly grew very cautious. 'I live around here,' he said, and then added. 'A lot of the *Daoine Sidhe* live around here.'

'Why?' Donal asked.

'Because it's a very special place. It's very ancient; there was a fairy-fort here long before the town of Bannow was built.'

'What happened to the town?' Donal asked.

The leprechaun turned his back on the children and looked out over the low mounds and ridges which marked the old town halls. He shook his head slowly. 'I can remember when this was a rich, flourishing town, and before that I can remember the rich pasturelands, and before that I can remember the old De Danann fort that used to be here. But that was a long time ago,' he said, turning back.

'Tell us what happened,' Susan begged, and the twins said, 'Yes, please do.'

Donn Dearg hesitated for a few moments and then he sat down on the stones beside them. 'I can only stay a few minutes,' he said, 'but I'll try.' The small wizened man pulled out a long white pipe and quickly filled it with a fine green tobacco. He whispered a word and touched the end of his finger to the bowl and immediately began to puff thick clouds of smoke.

'How did you do that?' Simon asked in a whisper.

Donn Dearg smiled and winked. 'Magic,' he said, and began his tale. 'The town of Bannow was built on the site of a fairy fort. Now, while the *Daoine Sidhe* didn't like this there was little they could do without drawing attention to themselves – and the fairy-folk do not like to draw attention to themselves. So they held a great council and decided that if the Human-Folk did nothing to disturb them, they would leave them in peace.

'And so they did for a while.

'But then the Human-Folk discovered that there was precious metal in the ground around their town, and so they began to dig down into the earth. Well, the *Sidhe* couldn't allow that now, could they?' Donn Dearg asked.

'Why not?' Susan wondered.

'Why not? Because they live in the ground, little lady, and how would you like some giant digging a great big hole in the roof of your house?'

The twins giggled at the thought of a giant digging a hole in the roof of their house in Chelsea, but Donn Dearg shook his head. 'It's not funny, you know.'

Donal shushed them. 'Go on,' he said to the leprechaun.

'Well ...' said Donn Dearg, and puffed angrily on

72

his pipe, sending clouds of white smoke up into the clear blue sky.

'Well, all the fairy-folk gathered together on the beach down there, and, with the help of some of the Sea-Folk, they worked a piece of the Old Magic.'

'What's Old Magic?' Simon asked.

'The most powerful kind in the world,' Donn Dearg said. 'Anyway, they worked some of the Old Magic and from that night onwards the fairy-folk have been slowly covering the town with sand, burying it deeper and deeper. In a few hundred years there will be nothing left, nothing at all.'

'I wonder what it looked like,' Susan said quietly, looking out over the ruins.

Donn Dearg smiled sadly. 'It was nice,' he admitted. 'I liked it. In the morning with the sun shining on the white-washed houses it looked lovely, and in the evening, with the sun turning the thatch to gold, it was really beautiful.'

'I wish I could have seen it,' she said.

Donn Dearg looked over at her. 'Do you really?' he asked.

Susan nodded.

He looked at each of the children in turn. 'Would you like to know what the town looked like?' The three boys nodded. 'All right then,' the leprechaun said. 'Take hold of each other's hands,' he ordered them, and then he took hold of Susan's hand in one of his and Donal's in the other. The twins were holding each other's hands and Paul was holding tightly onto Susan's other hand. 'Now close your eyes,' Donn

Dearg said.

'What are you going to do?' Donal asked, alarmed now. He knew enough about the fairy-folk to know that they sometimes took children away with them.

'I'm going to show you Bannow from the very beginning,' Donn Dearg said. 'Now, close your eyes.'

Donal squeezed his eyes shut. He felt a cold breeze blow across his skin and ruffle his hair – although there was very little breeze that day – and then he felt the air change from warm and dry to warm and wet.

'You can open your eyes now,' Donn Dearg said. 'But keep holding hands – don't let go.'

The four children opened their eyes ... and found that the ruined church and the graveyard had disappeared. Everything had changed. There were trees everywhere, tall, thin trees that stretched up into the heavens, and short broad, wide-bodied trees that looked very, very old. There were holly bushes growing around most of the trees and, instead of the sandy soil, the ground was covered with lush green grass.

There was a movement amongst the trees, and then strange riders on tall, thin horses rode into the small clearing. They were wearing long grey cloaks that shimmered with the damp dew and beneath their cloaks they wore silver armour and carried swords and spears of silver. They stopped and looked around, and seemed to look right through the children and the leprechaun. More riders arrived and there were small, dark men with them that looked very like the leprechaun. The taller folk then gathered around in a huge circle, joined hands and bowed their heads.

A blue spark suddenly danced around them and then it shot out and touched the trees and bushes, turning them to dust. In a few heartbeats there was a huge clearing in the centre of the forest, with nothing but a pile of grey dust to show where the trees had once stood. Even as the children watched the dust shifted and scattered on the breeze.

More riders arrived, bringing supplies in broad big-wheeled wagons pulled by oxen. These brought stones, polished white, black and green marble, smooth slates and shales and glittering quartz. Soon a palace began to rise in the clearing. The *Sidhe*-folk used their magic to build a tall, strong fort of marble, roof it with slate and shale and use the quartz for the windows.

Time must be passing very quickly, because the four children could see the clouds racing across the sky, like a film speeded up, and they saw a wall growing almost magically around the fort. Then more riders came – but these were not like the ones they had seen at first. These were demon-folk, looking like huge snakes and each one only had a single leg, riding demon horses that looked like dragons. There was a battle, and the demons were beaten back. Again they came and again they were beaten back. The children saw the blue-white magic of the *Sidhe* battle against the red-black power of the demons. But the blue-white magic was stronger and the demon-folk were defeated forever.

Once again time slipped past very quickly, and the cousins saw that there were fewer trees now and they could see the blue of the sea sparkling in the distance.

There were new invaders now and these were the most powerful of all, because these were men and they brought with them a most fearsome weapon – iron. And the *Sidhe*-folk had no protection against the iron swords and spears of the men.

So the *Sidhe*-folk left the world of men and went to their Secret Places, the hidden forts beneath the ground, the floating islands in the sea, the Land Beneath the Waves, and the lost valleys.

Years slipped away quickly and the children saw the fairy-fort begin to crumble. First a few slates fell from the roof and then one of the windows fell out, and soon the great gate cracked and slipped from one hinge. Grass and weeds soon took over and then more and more quickly the walls began to crumble and fall to the ground, until eventually – although it must have been many, many years later – the fort was nothing more than a tumbled pile of stones.

And then the fairy-folk came back. There were only a few of them; two of them were tall and very beautiful – a man and a woman, and the others of them were smaller, darker people – the Earth-Folk. The Earth-Folk moved about quickly, shifting some of the stones and digging down deep into the earth, and then the *Sidhe* used their magic on the small hill. The ground heaved up and glowed a bright eerie green, and then a door opened in the grass and the children found that they could see down, far down into the earth. More and more of the *Sidhe*-folk came then and went down into the earth. Then the door disappeared, leaving no trace of it behind.

Time passed quickly again. Now a lot more of the trees had disappeared and the cousins could see the sea quite clearly. They found that there were ships in the harbour, tall square-sailed ships with many oars – and with a dragon-shape carved at one end. These were the Vikings. They had just started raiding the coasts of Ireland, robbing the towns and taking prisoners to sell as slaves, but now more and more of them were settling in small towns close by the sea. The Vikings built a town quite close to the fairy-fort, a rough town of wood and stone buildings, surrounded by a tall wooden fence with sharpened spikes.

Soon this town gradually disappeared and was replaced by a more permanent one of stone. The new invaders began to dig into the ground and began to mine a dull silver-grey metal from the earth. The metal was brought to a tall building in the town which seemed to be puffing out smoke day and night up into the sky, and every now and again, men would carry out boxes from this building, put them into the back of carts and ride away with them.

The town grew and grew, and then some workmen arrived with a small dark-skinned man in a rough brown robe. He seemed to be pointing directly towards the children, but the workmen just nodded and came over and started to dig. Very soon a building began to grow up beside the children. It was the church. The graveyard came next and soon spread out all around them. Bannow was now a large prosperous town, with many stone houses, and larger buildings in it.

The mines continued, and quickly spread further

and further out around the town, and very soon they approached the site of the ancient fairy-fort. Some of the men seemed to be objecting to digging near the mound, but others just ignored them and continued, and began to dig into the side of the fort.

In the blink of an eye the children found that a whole day had passed and it was now night time. To one side they could see the lights of Bannow town and before them they could see the fire of the watchman as he guarded the newly dug pit in the fort. But what the cousins could also see was the opening appearing in the fort above his head and two of the tall, thin people coming out. They looked towards the town and raised their arms and seemed to be clapping their hands. They then turned and headed off to the shore.

The forest quickly came alive with rustlings and creakings. The children saw the shadowy figures of small men, tall people, ghostly horses, and others heading towards the beach. From where they were standing they could not see what was happening down there, but they saw the streamers of light that shot up into the heavens, darting and spinning, spitting golden sparks and silver streamers down onto the town – but strangely enough none of the townspeople seemed to notice.

Time slipped away again, and now the children found that there were no trees left and they could see the sea quite clearly – only it seemed to be different. Was it closer or further away? It was hard to tell. But then they noticed that everything was covered with a fine layer of dust, and as time speeded up again, they saw the dust drift in over the town, first creeping up

78

along the walls, sifting through the windows and then covering the roofs. They saw some of the roofs cracking beneath the weight and crash to the ground. They saw the crops dry up and die in the sandy soil and, even as they watched, they saw the houses disappear beneath the shifting sand. And when they were covered, grass began to sprout on top of them.

The church remained untouched because the fairy-folk's curse had no power against it. But with no people to serve, it soon fell into disuse and then into disrepair, and it gradually crumbled away, leaving only a shell behind.

And now a fog seemed to come down, a thick, cold damp fog that covered everything and made it impossible to see even the hand in front of your face. The air grew cold and damp – and then suddenly it was warm and dry and the fog vanished – and the four children found that they were back beside the old ruined church with the sun beating down on their heads.

Donn Dearg let go of Donal's and Susan's hands with a sigh. 'That is what happened,' he said sadly. 'The townspeople shouldn't have tried to dig into the fort – but they were greedy, and their greediness not only destroyed them, but also their town.'

Susan pressed her hands together and rubbed them hard. She found she was trembling just a little. 'It looked ... it looked like it was a very lovely town,' she said.

Donn Dearg nodded. 'Aye, it was.' He stood up on a tall stone and pointed towards the ridges in the ground. 'High Street was there – Weaver Street over

79

there. The Upper and Lower Streets crossed there, and behind them was St Tollock's Street and then St Mary's Street came right up to the church. Down there St Ivory's Street ran into Lady Street ...' He nodded again. 'It was a lovely town.'

The leprechaun hopped down off the wall and turned back to the four children. 'I must go now, but thank you for your time, and for being patient enough to listen.'

'No,' Donal said, 'we should be the ones to thank you!'

'Yes,' Susan agreed, 'I don't think we'll ever forget it.'

Donn Dearg bowed to each of the four children in turn and then turned and ran off amongst the gravestones, finally disappearing down behind the tumbled stones.

When he was gone Susan turned to Donal. 'Was he real? Were we dreaming?'

'If we were then we were all dreaming the same dream ...' He looked around for the twins, but they had run off into the gravestones in the town, and seemed to be looking for something. 'Come on,' he shouted. 'We've a long way to go.' He turned and walked back towards the bicycles with Susan.

'You know no one is going to believe us,' she said.

'Don't tell anyone then,' he said.

'But people should know what happened here!' Susan insisted.

'We need proof,' Donal said. 'We need to be able to show them something from the old town.' He turned back and looked for the twins. 'Come on,' he shouted. 'Hurry up.' He looked at Susan's watch. It was nearly five o'clock.

They climbed up on the bikes and waited for the twins who were running through the graveyard towards them. 'It might have been a dream,' Susan said slowly. 'It's called a mass-hallucination.'

'A what?' Donal asked.

'A mass-hallucination is when a group of people all think that they can see the same thing.'

Donal looked unbelieving, but just shook his head and said nothing.

The twins came running up then. They were red-faced and looked as if they were both about to burst.

'What's up with you two?' Donal asked.

'You remember that tall building Donn Dearg showed us ...' Simon began.

'The place where the people brought the metal and then carried out those boxes later on ...' Paul continued.

'And you said that there was a mint here,' Simon said.

'Where they made coins,' Paul put in.

Donal looked at Susan and then nodded in confusion.

'Well, we were looking to see if we could find that building,' Simon began.

'And we did,' Paul finished. 'It was over there.' He pointed back across the field.

'So?' Donal asked.

The boys opened their hands. They were each hold-

81

ing a small round ancient-looking piece of metal.

'What are they?' Susan asked.

Donal picked one up and rubbed some of the grass and dirt off it. Underneath was a silver coin. He turned to Susan. 'People will have to believe us now!' he said in triumph.

Of course people didn't believe the four children. But they did have a hard time explaining away the two silver coins which the boys had found at the site of the mint, and it was even harder for them to explain how the children knew the names of all the old streets of Bannow ...

5

THE HUMAN HOUNDS

*FINN WAS AMONGST the greatest of the old Irish heroes.
He was a mighty warrior who, with the knights of the
Fianna, kept law and order in the land. He had many friends
both in this world and in the fairyland, but his constant
companion and most trusted friend was his huge war-hound,
Bran.*

*Bran was a magical beast, stronger, faster and more in-
telligent than any normal dog, and in a strange roundabout
way, he was actually related to Finn ...*

Tuirean was Finn's aunt; she was his mother's
youngest sister, and not much older than Finn himself.
She was a young woman of astonishing beauty, with
long, coal-black hair that reached to the back of her
knees, a small round face, and huge dark eyes. Many
young men fell in love with her and asked for her hand
in marriage, but she always turned them down.

Then one day Tuirean met a man called Illan, one
of Finn's captains from the north, and she fell in love
with him immediately. He was tall and handsome, and
his hair, like Tuirean's was coal-black, and he had fallen in love with the small bright-eyed beauty the first
time they met. But, because Illan was under Finn's
command, he had to ask his permission to marry

Tuirean.

Finn, Illan and the rest of the Fianna had been out hunting a gang of thieves who had been stealing from the villages. Around noon they had stopped on the bank of the river Boyne to eat their lunch and wait for the scouts to bring them news of the gang. Illan walked over to Finn and sat down beside him, resting his plate on his knee. 'I've something to ask you,' he said.

Finn, who was dangling his hot feet in the water, looked up. He was a tall, thin young man, with dark brown hair and the beginnings of a beard. But you could tell by his eyes that he was very wise, for they were the eyes of an old, old man. 'What would you like to ask me?' he said.

'I would like permission to marry,' Illan said softly, blushing slightly.

Finn smiled. He had seen Illan with his aunt over the past few weeks and he had guessed that this might happen. 'Would I know the lady?' he asked innocently.

'Aye,' Illan nodded, 'it is your own mother's sister, Tuirean.'

'My aunt,' Finn said.

Illan nodded. 'Your aunt. I love her you see,' he continued, 'and we wish to be married as soon as possible. And because you are my commander and since the girl's father – your grandfather – is no longer alive, I thought I should ask you.' He paused and added, 'What do you say?'

Finn pulled his feet up out of the water and began to dry them on the edge of his cloak. He glanced over at the older man. 'What if I should say no?' he asked.

The smile faded from Illan's face. 'Well,' he said uncomfortably, 'if you were to say no, then I suppose we would just run away and get married anyway. But I hope you won't say no,' he said.

Finn stood up and Illan scrambled to his feet. He put his hand on Illan's shoulder and the young man smiled warmly. 'Of course I wouldn't say no, and of course you may marry her – but only on one condition,' he added.

'What's that?' Illan asked.

'If I find that you are not good to my aunt, or that she does not like living in your fort, then you will allow her to return at once.'

Illan smiled. 'I will always be good to your aunt, and don't worry, I will be sending a messenger to my fort today with instructions to prepare it for my wife.'

Finn laughed and then shook Illan's hand in both of his. 'I hope you will both be very happy together,' he said.

'I know we will be,' Illan said.

Even as they were speaking, the scouts returned. They had come across fresh tracks further down the river and they had also discovered the remains of a camp-fire, which meant that the thieves were only an hour or so ahead of the Fianna. Finn hopped into his sandals while Illan ran off to gather up his belongings and pack them onto the back of his horse. Soon the knights of the Fianna galloped off down along the banks of the river Boyne after the gang. Illan couldn't resist laughing out loud. If they caught the thieves today, he could be back home by midday tomorrow and he and Tuirean could begin preparations for their wedding.

The day wore on. Finn and the Fianna always seemed to be just a little behind the thieves, and once they even saw them in the distance just riding over a hill. The Fianna had galloped after them, but by the time they reached the hill, there was a thin column of smoke rising from behind it, and when they rode over the crest, they found that the thieves had burned the bridge across a deep and rushing river. The Fianna were then forced to ride five miles upriver to find a spot where they could cross over without any risk of being swept away, and of course, by that time, the gang had disappeared.

They spent that night in a small forest not far from the sea shore. As well as the rich damp smell of the forest, there was also the tangy salt smell of the sea. Finn posted guards, because the forests then were dark and dangerous places, with gangs of bandits and packs of wolves roaming through them.

Illan was one of the guards. He picked a spot a little away from the roaring camp fire in a thick clump of bushes, where he would be able to see anyone or anything approaching, but remain hidden.

Back in the camp someone took out a harp and began to sing along to it, and Illan recognised the delicate voice of Cnu Derceol, Finn's favourite singer, who had learned to sing in the fairy-forts of the *Sidhe*. The men fell silent, listening to the beautiful voice, and slowly the night creatures in the forest stopped their creakings and croakings and twitterings to listen to the voice, and Illan saw more than one pair of small round eyes staring out of the trees and bushes towards the fire.

The night wore on, and the fire died down to glowing embers, flaky grey pieces of wood crumbling every now and again to send tiny red sparks spiralling up into the night sky. Soon, the only noises were the night-sounds of the forest, the gentle hissing of the sea and the snoring of the men in the camp.

Illan was tired. It had been a long day, and he had ridden far, and he was eager to return home to tell Tuirean that they could be married. He hadn't really thought that Fionn would refuse – but at least he had agreed without an argument, and everything was all right now. He began to wonder what it would be like to be married ...

Something white moved through the trees. Illan caught his breath and stiffened, and slowly, very slowly, he pulled out his sword. He waited, trying to follow the movements of the white shape through the trees. He wasn't sure what it was – but he was not going to call the camp awake until he was sure. He remembered when he was a young man shouting the alarm, and it turned out to be nothing more than fog weaving through the tree trunks.

The shape came nearer. Illan was nearly sure now that it was a figure – a human figure – but something stopped him from calling the alarm. Suddenly the shape seemed to melt into the ground, and then someone spoke from behind him.

'Hello Illan.'

He spun around, bringing his sword up to defend himself, but it got tangled in the bushes' thorny branches and fell from his hands. The pale woman standing before him laughed merrily.

'Dealba!' he said in astonishment.

The young woman smiled, showing her small, sharp teeth. 'So you do remember me,' she said softly, her voice sounding as ghostly as the wind.

'Of course I remember you,' Illan said, 'how could I ever forget you?' He shivered a little then, because Dealba frightened him, and Illan Eachta was afraid of neither man nor beast, but he did fear the fairy-folk – and Dealba was one of the *Sidhe*-folk. She was a banshee, a fairy woman.

Illan had met her a few years ago, when he had been doing coast-guard duty, watching the shores for any signs of pirates, or bandits attempting to land on Erin's coasts. They had met one stormy winter's night, when the seas had been pounding in over the beach, sending foam high into the sky, roaring and crashing like a hungry animal. When Illan had seen the white woman moving up the beach he had thought she was a ghost, but it was not until she was closer that he realised that she was just one of those very pale people that he sometimes saw in the king's court, and her white clothing made her seem even paler. They had become friends of a sort then; coast-guard was a lonely duty and Dealba was someone to talk to and laugh with. And it was not until later that he learned that she was one of the fairy women – the terrible banshee.

Illan suddenly realised that Dealba was speaking.

'I'm sorry,' he said, 'what did you say?'

Dealba frowned. 'I said that I heard that you have a new woman in your life now.'

Illan nodded. 'Yes, her name is Tuirean, and we will be married soon.'

'And what about me?' Dealba asked.

Illan shook his head. 'What do you mean?' he asked.

'I thought we would be married one day!' she said. 'You told me so yourself,' she reminded him.

'Yes, but that was before I knew you were one of the *Sidhe*. You know a human and a *Sidhe* can never marry.'

'You said that you would marry me.'

'I cannot,' he said.

Dealba's face grew cold and angry. The air around her grew chill and frost formed on the leaves and branches. 'You will marry me,' the fairy woman warned.

Illan shivered with the cold. His fingers and toes grew numb and he saw streaks of white ice forming on his armour and glittering on the metal of his sword, which was still lying on the ground. He bent down to pick it up and when he straightened he shook his head. 'I will not marry you,' he said. 'I do not love you.'

Dealba pointed her hand at Illan and said something in the language of the *Sidhe*. Immediately, the air grew even colder and then the leaves on the bushes around the man froze one by one, until they were like glass. The branches hardened and turned to a silver colour and Illan's sword grew so cold that it burned his fingers and he had to drop it. When it hit the ground it broke apart. The fairy woman took a step backwards and began to fade into the night.

'Wait,' Illan said. He didn't want the banshee to put a curse on him – he would never be able to get rid of it. He reached out for the woman and his arm brushed against a branch. The leaves immediately shattered and fell apart with a tiny tinkling sound, like small silver bells. Illan stepped backwards with fright – and touched against another branch. It too shattered into a fine silvery dust, and as the man watched the whole clump of frozen bushes collapsed into dust all around him with the sound of breaking glass.

Finn and the rest of the guards came running up, their swords and spears ready.

'What happened?' Finn shouted. 'What was that noise?'

'A banshee,' Illan said quietly, beginning to grow warm now that the cold had vanished. He looked over at Finn.

'She has cursed me; what will I do?'

'What sort of curse?' Finn asked.

'I don't know – yet.'

The captain of the Fianna looked troubled, and then he shook his head. 'There is nothing you can do but wait for the curse to catch up with you. When you know what it is you might be able to fight it.'

ILLAN AND TUIREAN were married a week later. The wedding was a huge happy affair, with all the knights of the Fianna and the nobles and their ladies there. It started at sunrise when the chief priest, the Arch-Druid, married them in the first rays of the morning sun, and then it went on all day, eating, drinking and dancing, and later on there were contests and games. When night fell, the bards came and sat around the huge fires telling stories about the ancient peoples who had come to the land of Erin. They told about the woman called Caesir Banba who came from the land of Egypt and who had given her name to the island; they told about the terrible Fomorians, who were demons from the icy north, and they told about the magical Tuatha De Danann.

After the wedding, Tuirean and her husband headed off to Illan's palace in the north of the country where they would have a few days holiday before he had to return to his duties as one of the Fianna.

However, only two days later, a messenger arrived from Finn, asking Illan to come back immediately. He said that a huge pirate fleet had been sighted off the coast, and Finn wanted all his best men by his side if they did try to land.

Tuirean stood by the tall wooden gates of the fort and waved at her husband until he had rounded the bend in the road and was out of sight. She was turning to go back indoors when she heard the sound of hooves. She looked back, thinking that Illan might be returning for something he had forgotten. But it was not her husband, it was a young man, wearing a messenger's cloak. He pulled his horse to a stop a few feet away from Tuirean and climbed down. He bowed.

'My lady,' he said, 'has my lord Illan set off yet?'

Tuirean looked surprised. 'He left only a few minutes ago – but surely you passed him just around that bend?' she asked, pointing down the dusty road.

The young man smiled and shook his head. 'I'm sorry my lady, I saw no one.'

Tuirean shook her head in wonder. Even if Illan had been galloping, surely he wouldn't have reached the distant crossroads so soon? 'Was there a message for my husband?' she asked then.

The messenger nodded again. He was a young man who looked no more than fifteen or sixteen, with a head of snow-white hair and sharp sort of face. 'I have a message for my lord Illan – and for you too, my lady,' he added with a smile.

'For me?'

'Yes, my lady. Finn fears that the pirates may land in some of the smaller bays around here and try and sneak south to attack him. He does not wish you to be caught out here with no one to protect you.'

'But the fort is guarded,' Tuirean said

'I think Muiren, Finn's mother and your sister, has insisted that he bring you south for greater protection,' the messenger said.

Tuirean shook her long jet black hair and stamped her foot in annoyance. 'Sometimes my older sister is worse than a mother – always fussing.'

'But does that not show that she cares for you?' the messenger asked quietly.

But Tuirean said nothing and stamped off to pack a small satchel and have her horse saddled.

A little while later Tuirean and the messenger rode

away from the fort and headed south in the same direction Illan had taken. They reached the crossroads by midday and then the messenger stopped. He leaned forward and pointed down one of the roads. 'That way.'

Tuirean hesitated. 'I thought it was this way,' she said, pointing down another road.

'We could go that way,' the messenger said, 'but this way is safer. It takes us away from the coast where the pirates might come ashore.'

Tuirean nodded doubtfully. She wasn't sure about that but she still followed the messenger down the side road. Soon they rode into a group of trees, short fat ancient oak trees with broad leaves and moss growing on the trunks. There was a little clearing beyond the trees and then the road continued on into a forest where the trees were growing so closely that their branches grew twisted together above the path and hid the sun and sky from their sight. Tuirean had to squint to see the path, and she could barely make out the shape of the messenger ahead of her.

Suddenly there was the sound of thunder overhead and then it began to rain. Hard heavy drops patted against the closely grouped leaves, spattering and splashing, but very few actually reached the ground below. The messenger raised his hand and stopped, but Tuirean was so close that her horse actually bumped into his.

'What's wrong?' she asked.

'Nothing,' the messenger said, 'but there is a clearing ahead and if we ride across it we will be soaked.'

Tuirean peered over his shoulder and saw what he meant. Ahead of them the trees had been cut away leaving an almost circular clearing through which the path ran in a straight line. She saw the rain then for the first time. It was falling straight down, drumming and thrumming onto the hard ground. Tuirean looked up into the sky, but all she saw were heavy full-looking grey clouds.

'How long will it last?' she asked the messenger.

He shrugged his shoulders. 'I don't know; not long, I hope.'

But the rain continued to pour down, soaking into the hard earth turning it to soft muck. Now water began to find its way down through the thick umbrella of leaves over their heads, and began to plink and drip onto the two riders, making them shiver and pull up their long riding cloaks.

'I think we should hurry on,' Tuirean said, pushing her long dark hair out of her eyes. 'We might be able to catch up with Illan.'

'Perhaps the Lord Illan is also sheltering,' the messenger said.

Tuirean nodded. 'That's what I mean. If he is sheltering from the rain, we might just catch up with him.'

The messenger nodded slowly. 'Yes, we might,' he said, but he didn't move.

'Well, let's go then,' Tuirean said angrily.

'Stay where you are!'

Tuirean turned to look at the messenger in amazement. How dare he speak to her in that way! 'What did you say?' she demanded loudly.

'You heard me,' the messenger said rudely. He urged his horse forward, out into the centre of the clearing, and then he turned the animal around so that he was facing Tuirean again. The woman was about to speak again, when she noticed something strange about the messenger – all the colours in his clothes, his skin, his hair – even the colour of the horse – were being washed away, running like wet paint.

Tuirean closed her eyes, squeezed them hard and opened them again. But the colour was still running down the man in long streaks. It had started at his head: dark brown streaks from his skin mingled with the brown from his eyes, ran down onto the front of his jerkin, and then the browns and greens of the cloth ran from that and dripped onto his legs. The colours then fell onto the horse's back and soon its brown coat was dripping away into a dark mucky pool about its hooves.

Underneath he was white – snow white, ice white, cold white. And 'he' no longer looked like a 'he' –'he' looked like a 'she'.

Tuirean looked at the creature and then felt her heart begin to pound with fright – it was a banshee! She tried to turn her horse around, but suddenly all the trees around her turned white with ice and frost. A tree cracked with the sudden weight of ice and sleet, and fell across her path, blocking the path. She turned back to the banshee.

'Who are you? What do you want?' she said as loud as she could.

The banshee smiled, showing her sharp white

teeth. 'I am Dealba,' she said so softly that Tuirean had to strain to hear her, 'and I have come for you.'

Tuirean grew very frightened then. 'What do you mean?'

'You married Illan,' the banshee said.

'Yes,' Tuirean nodded, 'I married him.'

'But he should have married me,' Dealba suddenly shouted. 'He knew me first!'

'But a human cannot marry one of the fairy-folk,' the woman said quickly.

'He should have married me!' Dealba insisted. 'But since he will not have me – I'm going to make sure he will not have you either!'

Tuirean managed to scream once before the banshee's ice-magic touched her. Dealba raised her hand and the air around her froze so that the rain which was falling close to her turned to snow and sleet, and the mud on the ground hardened into ice that cracked loudly. The banshee then pointed her fingers at Tuirean, and a thin sparkling line of white fire darted over and wrapped itself around the woman, spinning and hissing, crackling and popping. It lasted only a few moments – and when it had passed, Tuirean had disappeared also, but in her place was a huge coal-black wolfhound. It glared at the banshee for a few moments, and then growled deep in its throat.

Dealba laughed quietly. 'If Illan will not have me,' she said to herself, 'then I will not allow him to have you.'

NOW WHEN ILLAN reached Finn's fort, he found that

there were no pirates off Erin's coasts, and that Finn had not sent any messenger north for him. When he looked for the messenger who had brought him the message he could not be found. Illan grew frightened then, and thundered back to his fort, accompanied by Finn and some of the knights of the Fianna. They knew something was amiss.

When they reached the fort, one of the guards there told Illan about the messenger who had come with the message from Finn for the Lady Tuirean. And they had not seen her since then.

Illan raged and swore. He and the Fianna searched the surrounding countryside and he even hired men and sent them all over the country looking for his missing wife, but for a long time there was no sign of her.

Nearly a year passed.

It was high summer when Illan received a message from Finn. The Lord of the Fianna had heard a strange story concerning Fergus, one of the western lords. Now this Fergus was well known for his dislike of dogs, because he had once been bitten on the leg when he was a boy and from that day would not allow a dog into his fort. But what was curious was that Fergus had been keeping a huge wolfhound for the past few months, and treating it very well indeed. And what was even stranger was that Fergus insisted that Finn had sent the dog to him for safe-keeping. But Finn insisted that he had sent no dog to this man and wanted Illan to investigate, so the knight saddled up his horse and set off on the long road to the west.

He had ridden a few miles down the road when

something white flitted through the trees and stepped out onto the path. It was Dealba.

'What do you want?' Illan demanded.

The banshee smiled strangely. 'Where are you going?' she asked.

Illan was about to tell her but then stopped. 'Why do you want to know?' he asked.

Dealba smiled again. 'Perhaps you're heading into the west to visit Fergus, Lord of the Seashore?'

Illan felt a strange chill run down his back. 'How do you know that?' he whispered.

The banshee smiled. 'I know many things,' she said.

'Do you know where my wife is then?' he asked.

'I might.'

'Where is she?' Illan suddenly shouted, making his horse jump and sending the birds in the trees up into the sky.

'She is with Fergus, Lord of the Seashore,' Dealba said.

Illan knew then. 'And is she ... is everything all right?' he asked.

'She is in good health,' Dealba said and then added with a grin, 'Fergus has been taking very good care of her.'

Illan suddenly pulled out his sword and pointed it at the fairy-woman. 'You have changed her into a dog!' he shouted.

Dealba laughed. 'I have.'

'Change her back,' Illan said, 'or else ...'

'Or else what?' Dealba asked. 'I could turn you into

a block of ice before you had taken a single step closer. But I will change her back into a human shape for you – for a price,' she added.

'And what is the price?' Illan asked with a sigh.

'You must come with me into the fairy-fort.'

Illan didn't stop to think. 'Yes,' he said, 'I'll do it.'

Dealba disappeared in a rush of cold air, and then reappeared almost immediately with a huge black wolfhound by her side. As soon as the dog saw Illan it began to bark furiously and wag its tail back and forth.

'This is your wife,' the banshee said, and she touched the dog with the tips of her fingers. A white covering like snowflakes formed on the dog's hair. It grew thicker and thicker until the dog was buried beneath a mound of snow – and then it all suddenly fell away. And standing there in her human shape was Tuirean. She cried out with joy and ran over to her husband.

'You've saved me,' she said, 'I knew you would.'

Illan kissed her gently. 'But to save you I have to go with her,' he nodded towards Dealba, 'but don't worry, I will be back to you as soon as I can.'

'Must you go now?' Tuirean asked in a whisper, tears forming in her huge dark eyes.

'I must,' he said, 'but I will be back.'

Dealba reached out and touched Illan and he was immediately frozen within a block of ice. The banshee then touched the ice, and then both she and it disappeared in a glitter of silver snowflakes, leaving Tuirean standing alone.

A little more than a week later, Tuirean, who had

been expecting a baby before she had been turned into the wolfhound, gave birth to twins. But they were not human twins – they were two lovely wolfhound cubs.

Tuirean gave the pups to Finn to care for. The greatest magicians and sorcerers in the land were called in to try and give the dogs a human appearance, but they couldn't, because the fairy-magic was so strong.

And Finn named the pups Bran and Sceolan. They were magic hounds: faster, stronger and more intelligent than any other dog in the land of Erin. They were human hounds.

6

FINN'S DOGS

IN ANCIENT TIMES, it was quite common for kings of one country to send their sons to be educated and trained in another king's court. There were many reasons for this, but it also helped prevent wars. After all, a king would not be likely to attack another country if he knew his son was living there – would he?

There was even a time when Arthur, son of the king of Britain, and a distant ancestor of the great King Arthur, was sent to Ireland to be trained as a warrior and a leader by the mighty Finn MacCumhal, leader of the Fianna. However, the young boy very nearly started a war between the two countries ...

Finn MacCumhal stood on the hill top and looked down into the valley below. In the distance he could hear his men beating their shields and rattling their swords. They were making as much noise as possible to drive the savage wild boars before them into the valley where they would be trapped by the waiting hunters.

The tall warrior shaded his dark eyes and looked for his men. Luckily he couldn't see most of them – and that was the way it should be. His men were hidden in amongst the trees and bushes and if he could see them, then the boars, who would soon come snorting and

101

stamping into the valley, might also spot them.

However, Finn could see something moving below. It was a flash of colour. The dark warrior frowned; he had told his men to dress only in greens and browns, and not to wear bright colours today. He had seen the movement from the far side of the valley, where some of the young men he was training were hidden. Someone had disobeyed him. He pointed with one short stubby finger. 'Who's over there?' he asked, without turning around.

A man stepped up behind him and looked over his shoulder. He was Oisin, Finn's son, and was deeply tanned and as dark-haired as his father. 'Ah, that would be the young British prince, Arthur,' he said. 'I put him over there to keep him out of harm's way.'

'He's wearing something coloured,' Finn said quietly, although his son recognised the anger in his voice.

'Is it red?' Oisin asked, and then continued as Finn nodded, 'I told him to leave that cloak behind him.'

The tall warrior shook his head. 'That boy is more trouble than he's worth. I've a good mind to send him back to his father.'

'That might not be wise,' Oisin said quietly. 'At least while he's here, his father will not launch an attack on us, and, because the merchants know that there will be no trouble, trade has increased.'

'He could be a spy, sent here to find out our strengths and numbers.'

Oisin shook his head and smiled. 'I doubt it; he's too stupid.'

Finn nodded. 'Aye, I suppose he is. I've also

noticed he's a greedy young man.' He stopped then as a dozen and more large bristly pigs smashed their way through the bushes below. 'Ah! Here come the boar ...'

ARTHUR LOOKED UP when he heard the sudden crashing ahead of him. He gripped his long hunting spear tightly in both hands – and prayed that the savage animals would not come in his direction. Prince Arthur was almost twelve. He was a tall, thin boy with straw-coloured hair and very pale grey eyes. His face was thin and sharp, and his eyes were always moving, darting to and fro, and he never looked anyone in the face.

And, although there were princes and young lords from all over Erin, and from Britain, Scotland, the kingdom of Wales, and even from the lands further east, no one liked Arthur. He was a sly, secretive boy, who told lies and carried tales.

The crashing noise grew louder – and suddenly a huge boar broke through the bushes and stopped a short distance away from the boy. It snorted, its small black eyes as hard and as sharp as its two yellow tusks. Arthur backed away slowly, holding the spear out in front of him. He tried to remember what Finn had taught him about boar-hunting and about how to hold a boar-spear, but the sight of the huge animal with its bristling short hair drove everything from his mind.

The animal lowered its head ... it was going to charge.

Suddenly the bushes all around the terrified boy were torn asunder as three huge hunting dogs came crashing through them. They stopped and gathered around the boy, and for a single moment, Arthur thought they were going to attack him. Then he realised that they were facing the boar, standing between it and him.

'They must be Finn's war-hounds,' he said to himself, looking at the huge dogs, each one of which was easily the size of a small horse.

The three dogs began growling then, and Arthur saw their backs stiffen. With savage growls they leaped at the boar. It squealed once and twisted away through the bushes, with the dogs snapping close behind.

Arthur gave a sigh of relief, and then stiffened as he heard more sounds close by. A clump of bushes on his right parted and a man stepped into the clearing. Arthur recognised Ector, one of his father's warriors who had come to Erin with him.

'Are you hurt?' the warrior demanded, looking quickly over the boy, but, except for his pale colour, he looked unharmed. 'I saw the boars come this way ...' he began.

'I'm fine,' Arthur said, 'I think I frightened him off.'

Ector nodded, relieved. If anything happened to the prince, he, and the eight other men who had been sent to act as his servants and guards, would be held responsible. His father's instructions to them before they had sailed for Erin had been simple, 'Watch over him, take care of him, and do whatever he wants.'

'I thought I heard Finn's war-hounds coming this way,' Ector said, looking around.

'Ah yes, they raced through here just before you

104

arrived,' Arthur said. 'Tell me,' he asked then, 'just what's so special about those dogs?'

Ector leaned on his spear and ran the fingers of his right hand through his short grey beard. 'Well, you know that they're not supposed to be real dogs at all? Bran and Sceolan are actually related to Finn; his aunt had been changed into a dog ... or something.' The warrior shook his head. 'I'm not sure of the exact details. All I do know is that Bran, Sceolan and Adnuall are the finest hunting animals in all the known world.'

'Why hasn't my father bought them?' Arthur wondered.

'Because they're not for sale,' Ector said. 'Your father, and indeed many other kings and princes, have offered Finn huge amounts of treasure, cattle, and land for the three dogs, but he refuses to part with them. You see,' he said, lowering his voice to a whisper, 'they are magical animals – and there are very few magical animals left in the world now.'

'I'm sure my father would like them,' Arthur said softly.

'I'm sure he would,' the warrior agreed, 'but Finn is hardly likely to give them to him, now is he?'

Arthur smiled craftily. 'Could we not just take them?' he said, very quietly.

Ector looked shocked. 'But that would be stealing ...' he began.

'I'm sure my father would be very pleased if he got those animals as a present. He would be very pleased, wouldn't he?' he asked Ector.

'Well yes, but ...'

105

'And I'm sure if I brought him those animals, he wouldn't be able to send me back here would he?'

'No, but ...'

'So, if I bring him the dogs, I'll be able to stay at home, instead of here in this cold, wet country, where no one likes me.'

'Arthur, listen to me,' Ector said. 'If you steal those dogs from Finn, he will probably come after you for them, and more than likely declare war on Britain if he doesn't get them back.'

'Finn wouldn't dare! My father is the king of Britain.'

'Arthur,' Ector said gently, 'kings do not frighten Finn; nothing frightens Finn. I beg of you, do not even think about taking those dogs.'

But the prince shook his head stubbornly. 'No. I must have them.'

'I'm warning you not to!'

Arthur glared at the warrior. 'You have no right to warn me of anything; you have no right to tell me anything. I am Arthur, prince of Britain, soon to be king. I tell you what to do!'

Ector sighed. Arthur was one of the most difficult children he had ever met. He had a son of his own roughly around the same age, and the boy would never dare talk to any man that way. He could see why none of the other children liked the boy.

'I want those dogs, Ector, and I want them today. Now, listen to me. The hunt will be stopping shortly for something to eat. Everyone will be meeting down by the stream and while the men are eating, I want you to find all my men and have them waiting in the woods with fresh horses. Then you and that foreign soldier, the blond-haired one who knows a little animal magic ...'

'Olaf,' Ector whispered.

'Yes, that's the one. Find the three dogs, and have Olaf cast a spell on them.'

'What sort of spell?' Ector asked. 'You can't just make them fall asleep and carry them away. Have you seen the size of those dogs?'

'Well ... well, have him cast a spell of obedience or something on them.'

'It might not work – they are magical creatures.'

'It better work,' Arthur said, smiling to himself, trying to imagine the look on his father's face when he gave him the three dogs.

A LITTLE WHILE later, the short sharp blast of a hunting horn rang across the valley. It was the signal that the hunt was over for the moment and that some lunch was just about ready. One by one, and then in small groups, the men made their way out from the trees and bushes and down to the river bank.

Finn rode in with Oisin a little while later. He spoke briefly with some of the men, particularly with those who were new to the hunt, pointing out what they had done wrong, or indeed, how good they had been. At last he rode up to where Arthur was being served his meal by Ector, a little distance away from the rest of the men. The leader of the Fianna reined in his horse.

'I thought I gave instructions that no bright colours were to be worn today,' he said quietly, looking down at the boy who was still wearing his bright red cloak.

Arthur glanced up and then continued eating. 'I was cold,' he said at last.

'And very nearly dead too,' Finn said. 'If I hadn't sent Bran, Sceolan and Adnuall down to rescue you, you would have been torn to pieces by that boar.'

'I thought you said you frightened the boar off yourself,' Ector said, glaring at the boy.

'I did!' Arthur said sullenly.

'Do not lie to me, boy,' Finn snapped.

'They arrived too late,' Arthur replied. 'I had driven the boar off by then. Anyway, how do you know what happened – you weren't even there.'

Finn smiled coldly. 'Why, Bran told me of course. We will not talk of this now, but you will come and see me in the morning ...'

'I am prince of Britain,' Arthur interrupted, 'you can do nothing to me.'

'But you are not in Britain now,' Finn said, his voice growing very soft indeed, and all those who knew him knew that Finn only whispered when he was very angry. 'You are in Erin now, and you are in my care. I have a duty to your father to train you to be a warrior, and your father sent you to me because he respects me. In return I expect you to respect me, in other words, to honour me as you would your father.' Finn pulled on his horse's rein, and the animal daintily side-stepped. 'You will see me in the morning.' Finn then nodded to Ector and rode away, followed by Oisin.

Arthur glared after the two riders. 'You won't be seeing me tomorrow,' he whispered. 'Are my men ready?' he suddenly asked Ector.

The knight nodded, without saying anything.

'Let's go then.'

Arthur and Ector made their way down along the river bank, following the sounds of barking and yapping. They stopped before a huge clump of thorn bushes and peered out across the clearing to where Faolan the Hound-Master was feeding the animals and checking their paws for any signs of splinters or thorns.

'Where's Olaf?' Arthur whispered in Ector's ear.

'Here!'

Both of them jumped with fright at the sound of the rough harsh voice behind them. They turned around to find the huge northerner crouching down beside a tree trunk, grinning widely. They had walked right by him without noticing. He stood up and made his way over to the bushes without making a sound. Olaf was huge, even taller than most of the Fianna. He had bright blue eyes and he wore his blond hair in two long plaits down his back. There was an enormous battle-axe slung over his shoulder.

'What do you want me to do?' he asked the boy in his strange accent.

'I want those three dogs,' Arthur said pointing to Bran, Sceolan and Adnuall, who were sitting a little apart from the rest of the dogs devouring a huge bone between them.

'Good dogs,' Olaf murmured, pulling at his beard. 'Good dogs,' he said again, 'the best I've seen. Why do you want them?'

'As a gift for my father,' Arthur said quickly. 'Now, what I want you to do is cast some sort of spell over them, something that will make them follow you.'

The huge man shook his head. 'That might be difficult. There is a lot of magical blood in them – they might not follow me, and besides, even if we do get them, Finn and the Fianna will come after us. We wouldn't have a chance of escaping.'

'They won't follow us to Britain,' Arthur said.

'I wouldn't be too sure of that,' Ector said doubtfully.

'Finn would probably follow those dogs into the Otherworld.'

'We must hurry; the hunt will be starting soon,' Arthur said to Olaf. 'Now you, Ector must distract the Hound-Master.'

'How?'

'I don't know. Talk to him or something.'

'And what do I do if he won't be distracted?' Ector asked.

'Well then knock him out. But hurry, hurry!'

While Ector crept back through the bushes so that he could walk up the path to Faolan, Olaf began casting his spell. First he took a small leather bag from around his neck and, after clearing a space on the ground, tipped everything in it onto the clearing. Arthur, who had been peering over his shoulder and had been expecting to see something marvellous, was disappointed to find that there seemed to be nothing more than a series of polished white sticks.

'These are the bones of all the hunting animals that walk in these lands,' Olaf said quietly. 'Everything from the largest wolf to the smallest rat is here.'

'What are those markings there?' Arthur asked pointing to the scratches on the bones.

'They are Runes. It is a form of writing, something like your Ogham writing. But this is magical. Now watch. First we pick the bones for a dog, and I suppose I should use those for a wolf also,' he added, picking out two tiny bones and setting them to one side. 'Now we do this ...'

There were voices from the other side of the bushes as Ector wandered up to Faolan. 'A fine hunt so far eh?'

'Yes, very fine.'

'Your animals are magnificent.'

'Ah yes; they are the finest in all the known world, I dare say.'

The Runes had now been set out and arranged in a certain way, so that they formed a rough star shape, pointing inwards to the wolf and dog bones which were crossed in the middle. As Arthur watched, Olaf spread his broad hands over the design, closed his eyes and began to mutter in his strange language. For a while nothing seemed to happen, and then the prince saw a strange reddish-black glow seeping out from between the northerner's fingers. Suddenly, Olaf open-ed his eyes and looked at Arthur – and the boy nearly screamed aloud, because Olaf's bright blue eyes had turned into two red-black coals.

The huge warrior stood up and, raising his right

111

hand, he pointed towards the three dogs with his first and little fingers.

But the sudden sound made Faolan turn around. He stopped in amazement at the sign of the huge man with the burning eyes pointing at his three prize dogs, and then he reached for his sword. 'You ... !' he began, and stopped when the northerner's head turned slowly and looked at the Hound-Master.

'Get away from those dogs,' Faolan shouted and he began to charge at him with his raised sword.

Olaf pointed his finger at the Hound-Master, and a thin red-black spark hopped from its tip to the point of Faolan's sword. The sword was suddenly snatched from the man's hand and spun through the air, and then it embedded itself in the soft earth, where it began to melt into a pool of molten metal.

Faolan looked at the bubbling pool on the ground for a horrified moment and then he scrambled for his hunting horn. He had raised it to his lips when Ector struck him from behind, knocking him unconscious.

However, all the dogs had been disturbed by the magic, and began to bark and howl. Suddenly Bran, Sceolan and Adnuall leaped up and charged toward the northerner, howling like demons, their long yellow fangs bared.

Olaf pointed at the nearest dog, Sceolan, and once more a thin red-black spark hopped from his finger towards the animal. It seemed to buzz around the dog for a few heartbeats and then it jumped onto his coat and disappeared. Suddenly the dog's long-haired coat seemed to take on a life of its own, and stood straight out from his body – and then the dog stopped still, frozen in place.

The second animal, Adnuall, having seen what had just happened, dived into the bushes, and Olaf's red-black spark missed the dog by a fraction and fastened onto a bush. The bush hummed softly, as if a swarm of bees were trapped inside, and then it slowly turned into a pile of fine grey ash.

But Olaf's second try didn't miss and, like Sceolan, Adnuall froze into position with the hair in his coat standing on end.

Now only Bran remained. But Bran was the smartest of the three dogs. The northerner's first spark missed him, and turned another bush to ash, and his second spark struck a tree. Arthur and Ector watched fascinated as the bark of the tree quickly turned grey, and then this grey mould raced up along the branches and out into the leaves, and then, with a soft whispering sound, the tree crumbled to dust.

Bran knew that he couldn't hope to escape for long if he remained hidden amongst the trees and bushes, but there was the river. If he could get into the water, Olaf's magic might not work then; Bran knew that a lot of magic wouldn't work on water.

The dog raced through the woods towards the river bank, while behind him, bush after bush, and tree after tree turned to piles of grey dust. But there was water ahead of him now, he could see it gleaming blue and sparkling through the trees ...

Bran dived into the water ... just as the northerner's spark touched him. And then it seemed as if the whole river had gone mad. The water began to bubble and boil, and fish of all shapes and sizes jumped wriggling up into the air, and flopped onto the river bank, frozen into position.

But Bran too had been caught by the magic, and was now stuck half-in and half-out of the water, with only the back half of his body showing, his head under water.

'Quick, quick, before he drowns,' Arthur shouted at Olaf.

The warrior slowly shook his head and the red-black glow died from his eyes, returning them to blue. However, now the northerner looked pale and tired, as if the magic had drained him. 'Come Bran, come,' he said wearily, 'come to me.'

For a moment nothing happened, and Arthur was just beginning to think that Olaf's magic had failed, when the dog's legs quivered, and it slowly heaved itself out of the water, turned around and came trotting slowly over to them.

'Come Sceolan, come Adnuall,' Olaf called, and the two dogs also trotted over to him. 'Sit,' he commanded, and they sat. Olaf looked down at the prince. 'We have them,' he said.

Arthur looked at the dogs and smiled. They looked exactly the same as they had before – only now their eyes were a deep red-black. 'We have them,' he said. 'Come on, we better go before Finn and his knights get here.'

'THERE'S BEEN MAGIC worked here,' Finn said, a few

114

moments later when he and Oisin, with the rest of the Fianna came running into the clearing. 'I can taste magic on the air.'

'But what happened?' his son asked, looking around at the great piles of grey dust.

Finn sucked his thumb as he looked around, and as he did so, his eyes became distant, as if he were looking at something only he saw. At last he took his thumb out of his mouth, and said, so softly that only Oisin, who was standing beside him, heard. 'Magic. I see magic – animal magic, fire-magic, powerful magic, taming-magic ... '

'Taming-magic?' Oisin asked quietly, 'What is taming-magic?'

His father shook his head. 'Old magic ... old magic ... red magic ... northern magic ... animal magic. Animals!' He suddenly shouted, turning to Oisin. 'Count the dogs! Where are Bran, Sceolan and Adnuall?'

Oisin looked around in surprise. He knew he had missed something; it was the familiar three huge dogs.

One of the knights of the Fianna brought Faolan to Finn.

The Hound-Master was holding his head, and looked pale and sick.

'What happened?' Finn asked gently.

'I'm not sure,' Faolan said, shaking his head, and then wishing he hadn't. 'First, there was a man – a stranger by his voice – and he seemed eager to talk. And then ... and then ... and then there was another man,' the Hound-Master said slowly, 'but bigger this time, a giant of a man, with long blond hair, and a pale beard – and red eyes.'

'Red eyes?' Oisin asked.

'Yes, red eyes, eyes of fire. He pointed a finger at me, and my sword flew from my hand ... and melted into the ground. And then ... and then I don't know. Someone hit me; the first man I think. I can't remember. I'm sorry, my Lord; it's my fault the three best hounds in Erin have been lost.'

'No, it's not your fault,' Finn said quickly. 'I'm sure you did the best you could. Besides, there was little you could do against magic.'

'But who would have taken them?' Faolan asked. 'Who would be so stupid?'

'Oh, I have a very good idea,' the leader of the Fianna said in a whisper. 'Come, Oisin, we have work to do,' he said, walking away.

Oisin followed his father down to the river bank. When they were away from the clearing with its howling dogs and shouting men, Finn sat down on a tree stump and stared out across the water. His son sat down by his feet.

'Well, who do you think ... ?' Finn asked.

'Well, the man with the strange accent might be Ector, and the huge man with the blond hair and beard can only be Olaf – although Olaf has bright blue eyes.'

'But animal-magic is sometimes call red-magic,' his father said quietly.

'Would it give the magician red-eyes?'

Finn nodded without saying a word.

'Both Ector and Olaf are Prince Arthur's men,' Oisin said softly.

116

Finn nodded again. 'I know.'

'But why would he even attempt to steal the dogs?' Oisin asked in amazement. 'Surely he knows he can't get far?'

Finn sucked his thumb for a few moments, calling up the magic of the Salmon of Knowledge. 'Arthur thinks that if he gives the three dogs as a present to his father, then the king will bring him home from Erin.'

'And will he?'

'Of course not. If Arthur gives him the dogs, the king will just send them right back to me. He doesn't want a war with the Fianna Erin.'

'But will the boy give the dogs to his father?' Oisin asked then.

Finn smiled and nodded. 'Ah, that is a good question. Arthur is greedy, and that greed might trap him. He knows there is nothing like Bran, Sceolan and Adnuall in the whole world. It is my guess that once he reaches Britain's shores, he will probably hunt with the animals just to test them. Once he does that and sees how powerful they are and, more importantly, how powerful they make him, he won't give them up. You know Oisin,' Finn said, looking at his son, 'with those three dogs alone, you could defeat an army.

'We have to get them back.'

'I know,' the leader of the Fianna said wearily.

'Where are they now?' Oisin asked.

Finn sucked his thumb again. 'They are on board a small craft skimming across the waves towards Britain's shores. Arthur is there, with all his men – and the three dogs.'

117

'It must be a magical craft then if it's moving so fast with all that weight,' Oisin said.

'No ... no, strangely enough, it's not a magical craft. Ah,' he said then, 'the northerner has called up a magical breeze to push them along.'

'Well then, I'll go after them,' Oisin said quickly, jumping to his feet. 'Can you call up a wind for me and my men?'

'Better than that, I can call up a wind and Ferdoman the Half-*Sidhe* can call up a magical wave. One will push you along, and the second will carry you. They might land in Britain before you, but you will not be far behind.'

'Right,' Oisin said, 'I'll get my brothers, Raighen and Fainche.'

'Bring Faolan,' Finn said. 'He is the only one the dogs will go to, and I suppose you should bring Goll also, just in case you have to fight that northern giant.'

'We'll bring Bran, Sceolan and Adnuall back, father.'

Finn looked at his son and nodded.

SOON A SMALL wood-and-leather craft was skimming its way across the waves, its broad, square sail bulging before a stiff breeze. Oisin sat in the front of the craft, while Raighen, Fainche and Faolan sat in the middle of the boat. Goll – whose nickname was Mountain, because of his huge size – sat at the back of the craft, and he was so heavy that Oisin's end of the boat was actually up out of the water.

'Can you see anything yet?' Goll rumbled.

'Nothing but the sea,' Oisin said.

'Are you sure we're going in the right direction?' Goll asked.

'No!'

Goll sat up straight and very nearly capsized the craft.

'What ... ?' he began.

'We're going in the direction my father told the wind and the waves to take us. I'm sure it's the right direction. Now, stop worrying, we'll get there.'

'Well, I hope so,' Goll grumbled, 'I don't like the water; it's always wet and cold and it gets in my ears and up my nose.'

'Oh, don't be such a moan,' Faolan snapped. He had a terrible headache, and he was in no mood for Goll's moans and groans. The huge man always had something to grumble about, and yet he was one of the kindest of the Fianna, and also one of its bravest warriors.

'I see something,' Oisin said suddenly. 'Something grey, like a cloud, but it's not cloud.'

'Land,' Goll said, with a satisfied smile.

Almost as if the boat sensed the land, it seemed to pick up speed and soon it was almost flying over the choppy waves in towards the rocky shore.

'I hope this knows how to stop!' Goll said with a squeak of alarm as they approached the beach much too fast.

Suddenly the boat stopped. It didn't hit anything, it just stopped dead. Oisin, who had been leaning out over the edge, was thrown head first into the water, while Raighen and Fainche, his two brothers, were also tossed over the side. Goll, who had been holding tightly onto the sides of the craft, was also thrown overboard – still clutching two handfuls of crushed wood. Only Faolan remained in the boat, and he was tossed about, knocking his head again. He sat up, holding his head in both hands, and looked around. He was dizzy, and had a terrible pain in his head. 'I wish I hadn't come,' he said, with a groan.

A FEW MILES inland, Arthur, his nine knights and the three dogs were resting at the foot of a low rounded hill. Olaf's magical breeze had run out just as they sighted the shore, and the warriors had had to row their way inland, using their flat shields as oars. Once they had reached the beach, they had hurried away inland, knowing that either Finn or some of the Fianna would be close behind. However, they had to carry Olaf, who was exhausted from calling up the magical wind so soon after his animal magic, and this slowed them down. But, even though the northern sorcerer was exhausted, his spell continued to hold, and the three dogs were still under his control.

As they sat in the shade of an ancient oak tree, Arthur turned to Ector, who was sitting beside him, leaning back against the rough bark of the tree. 'Are you sure Finn will send someone after us?'

Ector nodded tiredly. 'Without a doubt. I wouldn't be surprised to see them come marching over that hill right now.'

'But we are in Britain,' Arthur protested.

'You do have Finn's dogs,' Ector reminded him, 'and nothing means more to Finn than his dogs. I don't think he would get as upset if his son was kidnapped. Our only hope now is to get to your father's court as quickly as possible, and pray that he can protect us from Finn's rage.'

'Too late,' Olaf murmured, 'too late.' The huge man was still half asleep, and seemed to be dreaming.

Ector suddenly stood up, and pulled out his sword. 'It is too late!' He pointed with his sword.

The eight knights saw Oisin, with his brothers Raighen and Fainche, followed by Goll and Faolan, come charging down the hill towards them, their swords and spears ready.

'There's only five of them,' Arthur said with a grin, 'and there's nine of us – well, eight awake,' he said looking at Olaf. 'Nine if you count me. We should be a match for them.'

'Ah, but they are Fianna,' Ector said sadly, 'and no one is a match for the Fianna. We are all dead men.'

The battle was short and furious and Arthur's knights fought well, but they were no match for the Fianna, who were the finest warriors in the known world. Even huge Olaf – who had been awakened by the noise – was defeated by Goll, and as soon as this happened the red-black light died in the three dog's eyes. And then they too joined in the fight.

Soon only Arthur remained standing. But when Faolan was about to stab him with his spear, Goll stepped in front of him, and raised a hand.

'You cannot kill him; not yet anyway.'

121

'Why not?' Faolan demanded. 'His men knocked me out and stole my animals – and ruined one of my best swords also. I'm going to kill him.'

'But he is not yours to kill,' Goll said. 'He stole Finn's animals, and don't forget, Finn is also your commander.'

Faolan looked so disappointed that Goll had to laugh.

'But don't worry, I'm sure if Finn decides to kill him, he'll let you do it!'

Oisin knelt on the ground and the three dogs crowded in around him, barking happily and wagging their tails furiously. 'Come on,' he said, 'let's go home.'

However, Finn didn't kill Arthur. When he was taken back to Erin, he was made to swear a great oath to be one of Finn's followers for the rest of his days, and to pay him a tribute every year.

Some people were surprised because Arthur got away so lightly, but if the truth were only known, Finn didn't really care what happened to the boy as long as he got his dogs back and, by sparing his life, Finn had gained the undying friendship of the king of the Britons. During his lifetime there was never war between the two countries.

IRISH FAIRY TALES

Michael Scott

'He found he was staring directly at a leprechaun. The small man was sitting on a little mound of earth beneath the shade of a weeping willow tree ... the young man could feel his heart beginning to pound. He had seen leprechauns a few times before but only from a distance. They were very hard to catch, but if you managed at all to get hold of one ...'

Michael Scott's exciting tales capture all the magic and mystery of Irish stories and he brings Ireland's dim and distant past to life in his fascinating collection of Irish fairy tales.

IRISH ANIMAL
TALES

Michael Scott

'Have you ever noticed how cats and dogs sometimes sit up and look at something that is not there?
Have you ever seen a dog barking at nothing? And
have you ever wondered why? Perhaps it is
because the animals can see the fairy folk coming
and going all the time, while humans can only see
the little people at certain times ...'

This illustrated collection of Michael Scott's
strange stories reveal a wealth of magical creatures
that inhabit Ireland's enchanted animal kingdom.
The tales tell of the king of the cats, the fox and the
hedgehog, the dog and the leprechaun, March,
April and the Brindled Cow, the cricket's tale ... a
collection to entrance readers, both young and old.

IRISH HERO TALES

Michael Scott

When we think of heroes we think of brave knights on horseback, wearing armour and carrying spears and swords. They do battle with demons and dragons, evil knights and magicians. But there are other kinds of heroes: heroes we never hear about.

IRISH FOLK STORIES FOR CHILDREN

T. Crofton Croker

These exciting and spell-binding stories are full of magical people and enchanted places which will delight and entertain children of all ages. *Irish Folk Stories for Children* are tales of past centuries when magic and mystery were part of everyone's life. They include such well-loved stories as 'The Giant's Stairs', 'The Legend of Bottle-Hill' and 'Soul Cages'.

FIONN MACCUMHAIL AND THE BAKING HAGS

Edmund Lenihan

Fionn MacCumhail and his companions might manage the usual run of everyday terrors – dragons, giants, monster moths and such – but they had precious little answer to the forces of the Dark. For this they had to rely on the knowledge and skills of the druids, especially the High King's own druid, Taoscán MacLiath.

But will he be powerful enough when the wrath of the terrible sisters, Adahbh and Eibhliú, the baking hags, is drawn down on the people of Ireland by a careless error during the building of the new royal highway to the west? It appears that even Taoscán's power may not be enough.

TALES OF IRISH ENCHANTMENT

Patricia Lynch

Patricia Lynch brings to this selection of classical Irish folktales for young people all the imagination and warmth for which she is renowned.

There are seven stories here: Midir and Etain, The Quest of the Sons of Turenn, The Swan Children, Deirdre and the Sons of Usna, Labra the Mariner, Cuchulainn – The Champion of Ireland and The Voyage of Maeldun.

They lose none of their original appeal in the retelling and are as delightful today as when they were first told.

The stories are greatly enhanced by the immediacy and strength of Frances Boland's imaginative drawings.

ENCHANTED IRISH TALES

Patricia Lynch

Enchanted Irish Tales tells of ancient heroes and heroines, fantastic deeds of bravery, magical kingdoms, weird and wonderful animals ... This new illustrated edition of classical folktales, retold by Patricia Lynch with all the imagination and warmth for which she is renowned, rekindles the age-old legends of Ireland, as exciting today as when they were first told. The collection includes:

* Conary Mór and the Three Red Riders
* The Long Life of Tuan Mac Carrell
* Finn Mac Cool and Fianna
* Oisin and the Land of Youth
* The Kingdom of the Dwarfs
* The Dragon Ring of Connla
* Mac Datho's Boar
* Ethne